Stranger in the Shadows

Books by Charles Mills

The Shadow Creek Ranch Series
1. *Escape to Shadow Creek Ranch*
2. *Mystery in the Attic*
3. *Secret of Squaw Rock*
4. *Treasure of the Merrilee*
5. *Whispers in the Wind*
6. *Heart of the Warrior*
7. *River of Fear*
8. *Danger in the Depths*
9. *A Cry at Midnight*
10. *Attack of the Angry Legend*
11. *Stranger in the Shadows*

The Professor Appleby and Maggie B Series
(with Ruth Redding Brand)
1. *Mysterious Stories From the Bible*
2. *Amazing Stories From the Bible*
3. *Love Stories From the Bible*
4. *Adventure Stories From the Bible*
5. *Miracle Stories From the Bible*
6. *Heroic Stories From the Bible*

*Bible-based Answers to Questions Kids Ask About Love
   and Sex*
God's Special Promises to Me (Pacific Press)
My Talents for Jesus / When I Grow Up (Pacific Press)
Secrets From the Treasure Chest
Voyager II: Back in a Flash

To order, call **1-800-765-6955**.
For more information on Review and Herald products,
visit us at www.rhpa.org

Stranger in the Shadows

Charles Mills

REVIEW AND HERALD® PUBLISHING ASSOCIATION
HAGERSTOWN, MD 21740

The author assumes full responsibility for the accuracy of all
facts and quotations as cited in this book.

This book was
Edited by Gerald Wheeler
Cover designed by Willie Duke
Cover illustration by Joe Van Severen
Typeset:12/14 New Century Schoolbook

PRINTED IN U.S.A.

02 01 00 99 98   5 4 3 2 1

R&H Cataloging Service
Mills, Charles Henning, 1950-
    Stranger in the shadows.

    I. Title.

            813.54

ISBN 0-8280-1316-0

Dedication

To Dorinda,
the center of my world

Contents

Land Beyond
the Lights

The dark form drifted along the midnight alley like a phantom. Cold rain fell steadily, creating glassy pools on the rough pavement, hiding torn newspapers and discarded beer cans amid shimmering reflections of neon signs and streetlamps.

Pausing at a corner, the pedestrian looked first one way then the other, searching not for traffic but for other occupants of the deserted section of the city. Seeing no one, the figure slipped quickly across the intersection, hurried to a passageway halfway down the block, and dropped from view, following a crumbling flight of steps to a door hidden below street level.

The shadow in the stairwell fumbled with the lock. A faint click, and the door opened and then closed, leaving the alley empty except for the driving rain and the night. Above the entrance, a faded sign swung on rusted chains, announcing to anyone interested that they were about to enter a portion of a building belonging to the city of Washington, D.C. In letters etched in faded and peeling paint the placard boldly proclaimed: Police Department, Section 31, MORGUE.

The darkened subterranean room consisted of bare block walls and stainless steel examining tables. A rectangular window resting above the outside entrance allowed a dim, colorless light to invade the stillness, illuminating with a slow pulsating glare the scrubbed floor tiles and metal-topped trash cans. If it hadn't been for the marquee across the street, the chamber would have been in total blackness.

The visitor walked slowly across the room and stopped at a table supporting a cloth-draped body. A wet hand reached out and tugged at the covering, revealing the lifeless face of a young man whose beard, cheeks, and hair were still soaked from the storm.

"You had to stay, didn't you?" the stranger said, his words barely above a whisper. "You had to prove somethin', like you was tough. Like you was a man." The voice broke slightly. "Well, now you're dead. So, whad'ya prove? Nothin'. Except that you can die like everybody else."

Pulling the stark white sheet down a little farther, the speaker saw a tiny hole surrounded by a patch of dried blood on the shirt just above the left breast.

Light pulsing from the window brushed across

the visitor's face, revealing angry tears. "Why didn't you run?" he cried out, his words louder than before. "You could'a got away with us. You could'a made it back to the neighborhood, back to the warehouse. You saw the gun. I mean, that jerk was wavin' it around like it were a flag! Knives is one thing. You have to be up close, you know, hand-to-hand stuff. Everybody's got a fightin' chance. Isn't that what you's always teachin' me? But a gun can chase you down. It can kill you from a distance. You knew that. You knew you shouldn't mess with a banger who's got a gun!"

The visitor flipped the covering back over the motionless form on the table, hiding it from view. "So, what am I 'sposed to do now, Karl? Huh? What am I 'sposed to do?" He turned and walked across the dark room. "You're my friend, my *best* friend. We're a team, you and me. We're the best there is in this part of the city. Some people said we even look the same, 'cept I can't grow no beard like you." He paused, then continued, addressing the draped body on the table. "You take good care of me, like a big brother. You know? You teach me stuff. You teach me not to let nobody kick me around."

A muted conversation echoed from the hallway beyond the closed door over by the big sink. The boy stiffened, listening as the voices faded away.

"Captain Harrison said we'd end up down here if we didn't get our stuff together," the young man continued. "Remember? He kept saying, 'Hey

Karl, hey Jared, you two are gonna end up checkin' into my morgue if you don't stop facin' down bangers on your street.' Remember he said that? I guess he's pretty smart—for a cop. He figured out stuff pretty good, 'cause here you are. Now you're dead, and I ain't got nobody. Yeah. He figured it out good."

Jared closed his eyes and released a long, painful sigh as he brushed errant strands of brown hair from his face. The faded Redskins baseball cap he wore shadowed his flushed cheeks and deep-blue eyes. A thin, worn jacket hung from his shoulders, doing little to keep the chill from invading his slender, well-proportioned body.

He'd seen dead people before. Guys got hit a lot on the streets. Every night he'd hear the guns, sometimes close by, sometimes far in the distance. The sirens would arrive quickly because cops would park their patrol cars at the outskirts of the neighborhood in the evening, knowing from experience that someone was bound to be shot, or cut, or bashed before their shift ended. They knew they'd find a body or two lying by a curb or sprawled across the floor of a dirty apartment bedroom. That was life in the land beyond the lights, where the beautiful city with its monuments and government buildings ended and the streets grew dark and dangerous as the sun sank beyond the Potomac.

To the world, Washington, D.C., represented freedom's power and the hope of democracy. But it was a different type of power that ruled the midnight alleys in this capital city.

Tonight was no different than the others save for one fact. Jared had watched his best friend fall dead.

The teenager slumped onto a metal chair and watched the reflected light from the bar marquee across the street pulsate over the floor tiles. He lifted his hand and brushed the cap from his head, letting it drop to his lap.

He wasn't sure how he felt. Angry? Yes. Sad? He didn't totally understand sad, because he'd never known joy. He figured that if he had ever felt joy, even just once, he'd know for sure what sad was. The streets had only sadness. It was almost normal, like breathing, and sighing—and dying.

Leaning forward slightly, the young man studied the still, draped form resting on the table across the room. After a long moment, he spoke. "I'm gonna leave." The announcement came as if the dead body had been waiting for a response to a previously asked question. "I'm gonna go away, far away," Jared continued. "There ain't nothin' here in the neighborhood. You was all I had. Now there ain't nothin'."

The boy stood and walked slowly to the table, trying to find justification for his sudden statement. "You always said, 'What's mine is yours.' Remember? So I'm gonna take some stuff—from you and from the warehouse. It's my stuff now."

He pulled on the cover and let its soft, white folds billow at the dead boy's knees. "I'll need the keys," he said. "And I'll take the money from behind the bricks. Should be enough."

Jared slipped his hand into the jeans pocket of his friend and retrieved a small set of keys tied together with a string. Then he explored the back pockets until he found a thin wallet.

Suddenly, he heard voices in the hallway—voices that grew steadily louder.

Quickly he jammed the keys and wallet into his jacket pocket, pulling the sheet back over the prone form before stumbling through the dim light to the door. For a second he turned to look back toward the body. "I'm gonna miss you, Karl," he whispered. "You was my best friend."

He left just as the door across the room burst open, flooding the dim chamber with brilliant light. Racing along the rain-swept street, he rounded a corner and vanished.

Captain Joseph Harrison, a stocky Black man with friendly eyes and close-cropped hair, dropped a pile of forms on the desk by the metal cabinet. His companion, a man wearing a white smock, flicked on the overhead lights and jammed his fingers into tight-fitting plastic gloves as he crossed the room. Stopping by the body, he pulled back the covering and bent low to study the still face. "How old did you say he was?" he asked.

"Eighteen. Nineteen," the officer sighed, rummaging for a pencil. "Brought him in an hour ago. Gang-related. Guess someone didn't like his brand of deodorant."

"Any family?" The medical examiner saw the policeman shake his head. "It's amazing what a little hole can do to a big body," he mumbled, fingering the puncture wound. "Don't see any other signs of struggle. Fingernails are clean, relatively speaking. No bruises or abrasions visible. We'll do a complete workup as soon as my overpaid but thankfully incredibly lazy assistant gets back with the van. I mean, how long can it take to get pizza?"

Captain Harrison grinned. "Death make you hungry?"

"Yeah. Weird, huh?" The coroner chuckled. "So what's with this guy? Did you know him?"

The officer nodded. "Name's Karl. Karl Castanza. I watched him grow up on the streets. He was a nice enough person. Even tried to help people, taking in strays, you know, runaways with no place to go. He'd get 'em food, tell 'em to read books and not skip school. 'Course he also worked both sides of the law, and that's why he kept showing up here at the station handcuffed to one of my men. But we could never prove he did anything outstandingly bad, so we always let him go. Either he was really, really smart or we were really, really dumb."

"You were dumb," a voice called from the hallway. A second later outstretched hands holding a large pizza box entered the room followed by a plump, middle-aged woman wearing a rain jacket. The aroma of hot tomato and cheese blended with the faint odor of formaldehyde. "They didn't have any olives left," the newcomer announced, dropping the warm box onto an empty examining table. "I mean, what's pizza without olives?"

"A *good* pizza," the coroner said without looking up. "I hate olives. And what took you so long?"

"Why, Dr. Milton, sounds like you missed me." The woman blinked her eyes, trying to look seductive. "I was gone only a few minutes." She turned to face the captain. "He just can't live without me."

Harrison grinned. "You know, he *did* have that lonely, frustrated, lost-little-kitty look. As a matter of fact, he even mentioned that he felt you'd been gone far too long."

"See?" the woman declared, pointing at the police officer while looking at her boss. "Even our precinct captain can sense how much you love me."

Dr. Milton rolled his eyes. "Just get me a piece of pizza, Ashly. We can talk about my love life, or lack thereof, later."

Captain Harrison shook his head and chuckled. Ashly Peters had been trying to attract the attention of her coroner boss ever since she had transferred to Washington, D.C., eight years before. He was being as stubborn as she was determined.

Glancing past the pile of papers, he noticed something peculiar on the floor. "Hey, Doc," he said, "have you or Ashly used the side-street entrance during the past hour or so?"

Dr. Milton gently rolled Karl's body to one side and peered at the blood staining the back of his shirt. "Nope. We've been using the precinct entrance."

The officer rose and walked across the room, following a trail of wet footprints embossed on the black-and-white tiles. "Looks like we may have had a visitor."

Ashly glanced up from the pizza. "Someone musta stumbled in here by mistake, although I'm sure we keep that door locked. Whoever made the wrong turn had quite a shock when he or she realized where they were."

"He," the captain said thoughtfully. "Those are hiking boots, probably a size 11." Harrison stopped and turned. "Check his pockets."

"Whose?" the doctor asked.

"His," Harrison said, pointing at the body on the table. "Check to see if his wallet is missing."

Dr. Milton stuffed his hand into each of the four pockets of the victim's jeans. "Nothing," he said.

Captain Harrison frowned. "Karl always kept a wallet and set of keys on him. I've seen them enough times when he'd come in and we'd search him for drugs or drug paraphernalia."

"Maybe they were lifted at the scene, perhaps by the shooter," Dr. Milton offered.

"No. My men got there within 60 seconds of the gun going off. Witnesses say everybody vanished even before our friend hit the pavement. He just lay out there in the middle of the street alone 'til we got there."

Ashly tilted her head slightly. "So why would someone come all the way to police headquarters to pick the pocket of a dead guy?"

Harrison walked slowly to the door. "Not just someone. A very specific someone who is also very good at picking locks."

"Who?" Dr. Milton asked.

The police officer opened the door and climbed through the downpour to the top of the steps. The darkened street was empty, void of all life. Only the pulsating light of the bar marquee broke the midnight calm. Harrison glanced toward the corner and studied the shadows lining the buildings across the street.

Suddenly, realizing how wet he was getting, he turned, then stopped, staring at an alleyway beyond the intersection. A sad sigh escaped his lips as he watched the rain splash on the sidewalk. "Jared," he said, knowing no one heard. "Jared, I'm so sorry."

With that he descended the steps and reentered the building. He had reports to fill out, schedules to check, and a shift to complete. Understaffed and underbudgeted big city police departments didn't have time to deal with the broken hearts of young boys who'd lost best friends. However, he'd try to stop by the warehouse on his own time. He knew Karl's young companion would be hurting.

ℒ ℒ ℒ

Jared pulled the blanket up to his chin and stared at the rafters arching high overhead. He could hear the rough, crackling breathing of others in the big room, sounds to which he'd become accustomed long ago when he first joined "the gang."

A tired smile twitched at the corners of his mouth. The gang. What a joke! Unlike the traditional collections of egos roaming the streets, the gang of which he was a member consisted of the strangest ragtag collection of human beings he'd ever seen—old homeless men, poverty-stricken ex-factory workers, a few handicapped souls in wheelchairs, and even a college graduate who'd found himself on the guilty side of the law. They all lived at the warehouse, an abandoned building within a stone's throw of the Capitol.

Each day they'd head out onto the streets, panhandling the commuters around Union Station, begging on the steps of the Library of Congress, even asking hurried senators and political bigwigs for handouts beside the various government offices sprinkled about their section of the city.

Karl had served as their unofficial leader, offering rousing pep talks on cold, rainy days, encouraging each to "allow the good citizens of Washington, D.C., to be kind to you because it makes them feel noble." He was the one who taught them to be on the lookout for the various news crews buzzing about in search of a story. Members of Congress loved to be photographed acting gracious and tenderhearted to homeless people even if their kindness lasted only as long as the cameras were taping. Such an encounter was always good for a few bucks and the possibility of getting seen on national television. Of course, since there wasn't a TV at the warehouse, no one could be sure if their timid wave ended up on screen or in the network editor's outtake basket.

But Jared had other thoughts rushing around in his mind as he lay beneath the faded blanket listening to the rain brush against the high metal roof and broken windows of the large structure. He was leaving at first light. Unconsciously, his fingers pressed against the set of keys hiding in his pocket. He knew something the others didn't know. Karl had had one secret possession, a "Dream Seeker" as he called it, safely tucked away in another building nearby. No one else knew about it. Just he and Karl. It had been their secret.

A few weeks before, the two of them had taken their mystery machine out of hiding and raced through the dark streets, reveling in the delicious sensations of speed and power. But such excursions had been few because gasoline cost money, and money also bought food at the concession stands at the train station as well as "preowned" clothes at the Salvation Army by the harbor.

Dream Seeker was a luxury item they could seldom enjoy.

Karl had patiently taught Jared how to drive it, but there hadn't been much time for practice. "Someday we'll leave the city," the older boy had promised after a late-night ride. "Just you and me. We'll go to a place I know about, a magic spot far, far away. There you won't have to be afraid, and you'll see such amazing things, stuff you've never laid eyes on before."

To a 15-year-old those words held skin-tingling mystery and excitement. The very thought of heading out on a journey was enough to get him through a day filled with hunger and a night punctuated by gunshots and shouting.

Now Karl was gone, and he wasn't coming back. It was time to leave, and Jared knew it. Often his friend had said, "These streets have a way of eating young boys alive, of stealing their souls and their innocence." Karl had been his protector, his mentor, his friend. But tonight, in the blinding flash of a gun, death had snatched all that away.

Before the city awoke, before the other members of his group would miss him, before early-morning rush hour clogged the streets and interstates, he'd be gone, heading west to a destination he could only imagine.

Time and time again, Karl had promised that joy was out there beyond the city lights, where mountains touched the sky and the valleys breathed pure, unpolluted air. Yes, he'd go before the sun caught him, and he knew he'd never look back.

ぷ ぷ ぷ

Captain Harrison parked his pickup by the curb and surveyed the street thoughtfully. The warehouse loomed about a half block away, its neglected exterior faded and worn by seasons and time. The late-afternoon sun did nothing to enhance its appearance. Even though it had been washed clean by the storm the night before, it still looked old and neglected.

In some parts of the city wearing a police uniform marked you as an outstanding citizen worthy of respect and honor. But here, in the long shadow cast by the distant Capitol building, it simply marked you as a target. That's why Harrison had come dressed in jogging clothes and sneakers. His sweatshirt proclaimed in bright, bold letters: "Washington, D.C., a Capital City." Underneath in smaller print it asserted, "Be glad. We could be all be living in Los Angeles where they have crime, racial tension, unemployment, *and EARTHQUAKES!*"

The street was deserted except for an occasional taxicab hurrying by, its driver obviously happy to be watching this part of the city grow smaller in his rearview mirror.

A crumpled newspaper rolled slowly along the sidewalk, driven by warm, moist breezes drifting in from the Chesapeake Bay. Such was the autumn weather in the nation's capital—cold nights, warm days. Sometimes that trend would reverse itself unexpectedly, leaving commuters shivering as they hurried between workplaces and their trains and car pools.

Harrison locked the door of his small truck and dropped the keys into his pocket. He'd been to the warehouse a few times looking for suspects or "perps," as police lingo referred to perpetrators. They'd never found anything, but he'd learned of the odd collection of souls hiding behind its walls. He understood how they operated and how far they ventured throughout his city. And he also knew that this particular group of individuals were more interested in surviving than breaking the law, although it was common for some to do one to accomplish the other.

Striding quickly to the front entrance, he looked back at his pickup, hoping that in his absence it would remain all in one piece without sacrificing its innards to some chop shop or quick-fingered entrepreneur who could readily trade car parts for drugs.

Satisfied that the vehicle would be safe for a few minutes, he entered the dark confines of the structure.

"Anybody here?" he called out, knowing that

his shout would clear the area of those who'd rather not be seen. They weren't the people he was interested in at the moment. Harrison wanted information. That was all. He wanted to know where Jared was.

"Who's asking?" a deep male voice called from the far end of the expansive building.

"Captain Harrison. District police."

He heard a broken chuckle. "Why don't you just say, 'Hey, somebody shoot me'?" the unseen speaker declared.

Harrison grinned. "Yeah, like you guys can aim. I'm looking for someone."

"Aren't we all?" another voice said from a different section of the huge, high-ceiling room.

"I'm looking for a young boy. Name's Jared. He was a friend of Karl's."

A long silence. "We was all friends of Karl's," someone else said. "And we're going to nail the jerk that wasted him."

"I'm sure you are," the police captain stated, searching the shadows for a face. "Just don't do it on my beat. Take your war up past Florida Avenue. They've got better ambulances."

A rough, coughing chuckle echoed in the stillness. "Whadda ya want with young Jared?"

"Nothin'. Just wanna talk to him. I'm sure he's takin' last night pretty hard."

After another moment of silence, Harrison saw a lone figure walk from the shadows and stand backlit by the stream of light tilting down from a high window to his left. "He's strong. He'll get over it," the man stated without emotion.

The policeman nodded. "Sometimes a guy needs a little help."

The shadowy figure moved slightly. "Whadda ya gonna do, adopt him?"

Harrison smiled. "Already got a son. Just wanted to see if Jared's OK."

The figure moved closer, allowing front-angled light to fall on his face. Harrison saw an old man, skin lined by years of neglect, staring back at him. "Jared's special. He ain't like the others."

"I know," the officer said softly. "He's been protected. But now that protection's gone. The boy may need help."

By now the old man stood a dozen feet from the visitor. Shocks of snow-white hair jutted from a torn winter cap. "He gone," he said. "Left early this morning."

"Gone? Gone where?"

"Away. Took his bedding, his jacket, his bag, and left."

The policeman frowned. "He's on the street?"

"Sorta."

"Whadda ya mean, sorta?"

The old man moved even closer. "Can I trust you?"

"I'm a cop!"

"That don't mean nothin' 'round here. Can I trust you?"

25

Harrison nodded. "Yeah. You can trust me. I'm no saint, but I care about people, especially young teens stuck on the streets keeping company with the likes of you."

A smile cracked the scowl on the old man's face. "You said your name is Harrison, right?"

"Yes. I'm Captain Joseph Harrison."

"I heard Karl talk about you, about how you was OK for a cop, about how you could never get anything on him, but he figured you'd hand him a fair shake if you had."

The policeman nodded. "Karl was one of our smarter felons."

"Yeah. He was. He was smart, but not smart enough to run from a gun."

"Is that really the way it was?"

The old man's smile broadened. "Say, you are kinda smart for a cop, Captain Joseph Harrison. You know Karl wouldn't face down a gunman on the street. That'd be suicide."

"So?"

"So, you wanna know what really happened?"

The officer tilted his head slightly. "Is this off the record or on?"

He saw the smile fade. "They was after Jared. The bullet was meant for him. Karl put himself between the gang and his friend, and they shot him down cold, just like that." The man attempted to snap his fingers. "Karl sacrificed himself for the young boy, and Jared don't even know it."

A distant siren wailed and warbled for a moment. The two men stood facing each other in the dusty expanse of the warehouse. Finally, Captain Harrison spoke. "Do you know who pulled the trigger?"

The old man pointed to the window and to the city beyond. "Take your pick."

Harrison realized there was a lot of truth behind the old man's words. People died on big city streets for a lot of reasons. Poverty, desperation, lost dreams, the agony of waking up to face another day of neglect and rejection—all these factors helped hold the gun steady as the finger pressed the trigger. He knew his men might find the owner of the bullet, but they could never capture the devil that gave it flight.

The police officer shook his head. "So whadda ya mean by he's on the street, *sorta?*"

The old man grinned. "He got himself a Dream Seeker."

"A what?"

"It's supposed to be a secret, but I knew. Karl told me. He says to me, 'If anything ever happens, I got a way to get Jared out of the city.' And he showed it to me. Nice machine. All shiny. Lots of chrome. Real powerful—"

"What are you talking about, old man?" Harrison interrupted, a touch of impatience in his voice. "Are you telling me that Jared, a 15-year-old juvenile, has a car?"

"A car? No. No! Something better. Something faster." The speaker lifted his arms out in front of him and rolled his right fist up and down. "He's got a Dream Seeker, and you can't catch him. Varoom, VAROOM!" The old man roared out the sound of an engine from deep in his throat. "VAROOM!"

Other unseen voices joined his, echoing the sound of powerful exhaust throughout the building, the noise growing in intensity and volume. "VAROOM! VAROOM!"

Captain Harrison stood in the middle of the abandoned warehouse surrounded by the deafening roar coming from a dozen men's throats, shouting out the sound of escape, the sound of longing, the sound of the mysterious Dream Seeker.

🥾 🥾 🥾

VAAA—ROOOOM! A metallic streak of yellow and silver roared along a West Virginia back road, causing the leaves and bushes along the asphalt to flutter and bend violently forward, then return to their normal position facing the sun.

The rider leaned low over the handlebars, sensing the powerful vibration between his legs, marveling in the sensation of speed he'd experienced several times before when he and Karl had raced along darkened city streets.

His right wrist twitched, causing the machine to raise the tone of its whine slightly, propelling him forward at an even greater clip.

28

The world was a blur. Only the road stayed in focus while broken lines of white flicked by underneath in rapid succession.

Jared felt the warmth of the engine mixing with the cool, mountain air blasting past him in a constant, jacket-grabbing stream. Sounds were muffled, thanks to the tight-fitting helmet encasing his head and jaw. A clear, plastic visor covered his eyes.

He'd dreamed it would be like this, fast and free, with new sights waiting at every bend. But he'd never imagined just how alive he'd feel, hugging the sleek, shiny motorcycle, admiring the four pitch-tuned exhaust pipes extending from the broad engine and sweeping back, two to a side, past his footholds in the direction of the rear wheel where each tilted upward slightly, shouting their angry roar into the slipstream.

Was this it? Was this happiness? It felt so deliciously good, so heart-stoppingly fantastic, so sensual all at the same time. He was free—he was away from the city. At last he was safe.

Cresting a hill, he noticed a broad, empty parking area beside the road. "Grand Lookout" a small sign announced.

Gearing down exactly the way Karl had taught him, he slowed the machine and followed the arrows to the rest area. With a squeak, the motorcycle came to a complete stop, and Jared reached over and turned the key. The roar disappeared, leaving only a ringing, a wonderful, restful ringing in his ears. He sat for a long moment, feeling the silent machine under him as it supported his weight, holding him comfortably aloft, save for his left toes that rested gently on the graveled ground.

Transferring his weight to his right foot, he kicked the stand down and leaned the bike back to the left before swinging himself off. Walking slowly, he headed toward the stone fence separating him from the breathtaking vista of mountain range after mountain range stretching far to the west. The sun hung low over the horizon, waiting for night to summon it into darkness.

Turning, he gazed back at the motorcycle. Karl had stated that it was a Honda CB750, assembled many years ago in a factory in Japan. But Jared knew better. It truly was a Dream Seeker, a magic carpet of escape, a savior for young boys desperate to leave the city.

Reaching into his back pocket, he pulled out a worn and tattered brochure. The document had been safely stored with the motorcycle in Karl's secret hiding place. It told of a ranch far to the west where teens could find safety and acceptance. His friend had spoken of it with longing in his voice. "They got horses," he'd said. "They got mountains. They got trees and rivers. See?" He'd hold the brochure up for his companion to study. It had photographs of teens racing along meadows and climbing mountain paths. The faces were all smiling, all joyous, all satisfied. This was where he was going—where the Dream Seeker would take him.

Jared watched the last rays of the sun sink below the horizon. He stood motionless for a long moment, helmet tucked under his arm, drinking in the sight. Then it hit him. He was feeling happiness. For the first time ever he felt joy.

But, just as suddenly as those new feelings entered his mind, he felt terribly alone. Karl was dead. His best friend in all the world would not be making the journey with him.

In the half-light of dusk, alone on the mountaintop, the boy sank to his knees, clutching the brochure. Evening shadows lengthened about him as he wept, his young heart breaking. Now he knew sadness. He really knew it because, for the first time he'd experienced a moment of true joy.

Nearby, the Dream Seeker sat waiting, its engine clicking and snapping as it cooled in the night air. A small canvas duffle bag, containing his only earthly possessions, sat tied securely to the luggage rack. Inside were other brochures boasting of the beauty of a faraway horse ranch in Montana. In big, bold letters, each invited, "Leave the past behind. Find a new direction at Shadow Creek Ranch."

Night swallowed up the machine and the rider, drawing a silent curtain about the boy, hiding his sorrow in darkness.

CHAPTER 2

Escape-proof

Captain Harrison rubbed his chin thought-fully, feeling rough stubble scratch against his fingers. He frowned. Forgot to shave again. His wife was constantly nagging him to take the time to plug in his electric razor and relieve his face of its daily growth, an activity and piece of advice he ignored all too frequently.

A knock on his office door brought his thoughts back to the day's work. "Here's the autopsy report on the Castanza stiff," Ashly called with a smile. "Dr. Milton said to tell you that he has no doubt as to cause of death."

"And?" Harrison encouraged.

The woman dropped a folder onto a stack of papers. "The victim was shot."

"You know," the captain said with a sigh, "that's why you people in the morgue make the big bucks. You can see right through the suspicious and get directly to the obvious."

Ashly grinned. "We do our best. Probably a .38. No powder burns, so the gunman wasn't trying to be up close and personal. Our boy was dead when he hit the ground. Didn't find any drugs on or in him. Don't even think he smoked. Alcohol levels were OK. If he weren't dead, he could drive." The speaker paused. "Doesn't exactly fit the profile of your typical street bum."

"I'm discovering he was a very special street bum," the officer stated, glancing at the report. "Took the bullet for a young friend."

Ashly frowned. "I thought there was no honor among thieves."

"The street is full of surprises." Harrison sighed. "Thanks for the report and tell Dr. Milton to send the body on for disposal. Karl didn't have any family that I know of. I've done a computer search and made a few phone calls. As far as society is concerned, Karl Castanza simply never existed."

"OK," Ashly agreed, turning to leave. She paused at the door. "Captain, are you all right?"

The policeman glanced up from the report. "Yeah. I'm fine. Just tired. Too many late nights and soggy pizzas."

The middle-aged woman nodded. "I know what you mean. We all could use a good vacation. How 'bout it? Let's just close up shop and go to the mall."

"Sounds like a plan," Harrison declared. "But first, go out and convince everyone in Washington to play nice. Then we're outta here."

The woman groaned. "Yeah. Like that's going to happen. Well, there's no reason why you shouldn't take a few days off. If you don't mind me saying so, you look like someone me and Doc should be examining, not working with." She smiled. "You might wanna shave, too."

He grinned. "You must've been talking to my wife, both about the shaving and the vacation part. I'll be OK. Thanks for your concern."

Nodding, she left, closing the door behind her.

That evening Captain Harrison quit work early and drove through the crowded streets to his modest home in a subdivision just outside of Silver Spring, Maryland, north of the District. He liked the cracked sidewalks and thick, gnarled trees lining the avenues, their heavy branches echoing the late-day laughter of children.

Many years before, the real estate agent who'd sold him the property had labeled his particular section of town as "mature." Harrison knew that really meant "old." But it didn't matter. He loved the peaceful feel of the place even though his, and all the other houses facing the streets, had seen more prosperous days. Besides, mature also meant cheap. Police captains working for the city didn't need to spend much of their day searching for tax shelters or studying the *Wall Street Journal*.

"Luella? I'm home." Harrison slipped off his windbreaker and hung it by the door. "Thought I'd kick off early." He unfastened his holster and jammed his gun into the wall safe over the bookcase. "Is Perry back yet?"

A smiling face adorned with a set of soft brown eyes framed by dark curls appeared in the doorway leading into the kitchen. "Hey, handsome," the woman called, wiping her hands on her apron. "They said you'd already left when I phoned a few minutes ago. Are you sick? You don't usually come home so early."

The policeman swept the woman into his arms and danced her around the room. "I've come to take you away from all this, to carry you off on my noble steed to my secret castle in the sky."

"Terrific," the woman stated, eyeing her husband thoughtfully. "But can we stop by the grocery store on the way? I need some toilet paper and a can of beans."

Harrison grinned. "Beans and toilet paper. You're fixing Mexican tonight, right?"

Luella rolled her eyes and pulled away from her husband's embrace. "No, silly. I made me and Perry a bowl of soup and some sandwiches for supper which you're welcome to share as soon as he gets home. The beans are for tomorrow."

"But what about my castle?" the man asked, feigning frustration. "When can I take you away from it all?"

35

The woman thought for a moment. "Thursday. After band practice."

"Fair enough," the policeman chuckled. "Gives me something to look forward to. Perry will be surprised to see me, won't he? I mean, I'm not usually here when he gets home from school."

Just then the front door burst open and a tall, lanky teenager entered, dribbling a basketball as he walked. "Ma? I'm ho—" He stopped in his tracks, allowing the ball to bounce unaccompanied across the room. "Hey, what are you doing here?"

"This is where I live. I'm your dad. Surely you've seen pictures."

The teen shrugged. "What's for supper, Ma? I'm starved." He brushed past the man and headed for the kitchen, retrieving the ball along the way.

Captain Harrison watched him go. This was the way it had been for some time now. He and Perry seemed to be living in different worlds, moons of different planets, their paths crossing less and less frequently.

"Hey," the man called, trying to sound cheerful. "How 'bout us going out to eat? You know, Taco Bell? Something like that?"

Perry turned. "I don't have time, Dad. Gotta get to the gym for practice before the game."

"Gotta big game tonight?"

"Sorta."

"Hey, I'll come and cheer you on. I've been

practicing the wave." Harrison lifted his arms and let them drop again. "See? It kinda works better with more people."

"Yeah. Great, Dad. You can come if you want. Whatever."

Harrison stood in the entryway in silence, re-membering times when his presence brought shouts of joy and little chubby arms around his neck. Try as he might, he couldn't even remember the last time he'd hugged his son.

"I just want to be there for you—you know, dear old dad cheering from the stands. Didn't I hear you say you were going to be playing the eastern division state champions? Don't want to miss that one."

Perry adjusted his baseball cap and cleared his throat impatiently. "That was last month, Dad. We beat 'em 97-94."

The man's smile faded. "Oh. I see. Well, good for you. Guess I musta had an emergency down at the precinct."

"Yeah," Perry stated coldly, "like you always do. Gotta keep the citizens safe."

"Yes, that's right. It's my job."

"Well, don't let me get in the way of you doing your job. Why don't you call the office right now? There's probably somebody killing somebody even as we speak. Maybe even two homicides if you're lucky."

"Hold on there, young man," Harrison warned.

"People getting killed is no laughing matter."

Perry lifted his hand. "Hey, I'm not laughing. I don't do that anymore. Don't have anyone around to show me how."

With that, the teen picked up the ball and headed back through the entryway and out the door.

"Sweetie, how 'bout supper?" he heard his mother call.

"I ain't hungry." The slamming door punctuated his departure.

An uneasy stillness settled over the house. "What's with him?" Harrison asked, his voice strained with frustration. "What'd I say?"

"Nothing," Luella stated quietly. "We just haven't seen a whole lot of you for the past year—ever since your promotion."

"I can't help that. There's lots to do. People in the District keep messin' with each other. Somebody's gotta track down the bad guys and keep them from doing any more damage. It's my job to run the department. I happen to think what I do is important."

"And you do your work very well," Luella responded reassuringly. "But—"

"But what?"

"But you might try to spend a little more time with Perry. He feels kinda left out."

Harrison lifted his hands, palms up. "I keep a roof over his head, don't I? And he's not exactly starving!"

"No, his stomach's doing quite well. He eats like any healthy 14-year-old. But it's his heart that could stand a little attention. He misses his daddy. He misses the times you used to spend together."

The captain lowered his gaze and studied the designs in the carpet. "I do the best I can," he said.

"I know you do, honey. Perhaps you could do even better. Maybe you could find a few minutes each day to spend with him—just him. He's growing up and has questions only a father could answer. He's—"

RING! The urgent call of the phone interrupted the woman's words. Captain Harrison sighed and raised a finger. "Don't go away," he said, "I want to hear what you have to say."

The woman smiled. "I'll be here when you're finished."

RING! The policeman hurried to the phone resting on the end table at the far side of the little living room. He picked up the receiver as he settled himself on the couch. "Harrison here," he announced.

"Captain? This is Rodney. Hope I'm not disturbing anything."

"No, it's OK. What's up?"

"I mean, I know you knocked off early to be with your wife for supper and I—"

"It's all right, Rodney. Just tell me why you called."

"Well, Captain, something kinda weird has

happened, and I thought you might want to know about it."

"OK."

"I mean, you're not going to believe this."

"Rodney, just tell me what's goin' on."

He heard his coworker shuffling papers. "Well, we got a call from a constable in Ohio. You know that dead guy we brought in two days ago?"

"Which one?"

"Ah . . . Karl somebody."

"Karl Castanza?"

"Yeah, him. Well, we just got a call from a small-town police station in Ohio. Seems they picked him up for speeding."

"They picked up Karl Castanza for speeding?"

"Yup. That's pretty amazing, seeing he's dead and all."

Captain Harrison sat forward in his chair. "What else did they say? And why did they call us?"

"Well, Sheriff North—that's the officer who phoned—said they found a note in Karl's wallet that read, 'In case of trouble or accident, call Captain Joseph Harrison in Washington, D.C.' Our number was written below the message. So North phoned and wants to know what to do."

"What else did he say?"

"He said that Karl was doing 65 in a 45 zone earlier this afternoon. When his deputy gave chase, our guy gave 'em a run for his money. The officer pursued him clean out of town. He would'a gotten away 'cept our guy's motorcycle ran outta gas."

Harrison picked up an envelope resting by the phone and extracted a pen from his shirt pocket. "Give me the Ohio number, and I'll talk to this Sheriff North."

He wrote the information out carefully as Rodney dictated. When he finished, the policeman on the line asked, "Hey, Captain, how can a dead guy get busted in Ohio?"

"I'll explain later. And listen, don't talk about this with the guys at the station, OK? I'll take care of it. Thanks, Rodney."

"Sure thing, Captain. Have a nice relaxing evening with your wife."

As the phone went dead, Harrison released a long sigh. That poor officer in Ohio didn't know what he was up against. He thought he had a freshly shaven speeder named Karl Castanza in custody when, in reality, he was making his ID based on documents found in a dead man's wallet and the word of a fast-talking youngster named Jared. North also didn't know he was trying to detain a streetwise teenager who'd found his way out of more lockups than he cared to remember. Jared wasn't about to stay in Ohio one minute longer than he had to.

But where was he going? Most vagrants headed south in the fall, toward warmer climates. This lad was heading northwest, into cold country. What could possibly be on his mind?

With a plaintive glance at his wife, he placed the phone on his lap and began dialing. Luella smiled knowingly, shook her head, and headed back into the kitchen.

🐿 🐿 🐿

Sheriff North heard the phone ringing while he was in the ticket booth searching for a box of staples. His office, the pride of Stoneman, Ohio, occupied the old train station, a structure revered throughout the county as the building that once had a freight train run, literally, through it.

It had happened more than 100 years ago, but people still talked of the night when a fully loaded express, headed for the stockyards of Chicago, jumped the tracks and plowed through the loading ramp and waiting room. Since it was an express, and it happened at 2:00 in the morning, no one was in the building except the sleeping station manager, who woke up to find a collection of somewhat dazed beef cattle milling about his place of employment.

Years later, after the trains stopped running along the tracks fronting the rebuilt loading dock, the building had served as a warehouse, then a library, a restaurant, and finally headquarters of the Stoneman Police Department. Other than the fact that it had been the scene of the great cattle crash of 1884, the station boasted another first for the town. It had a jail. And in the jail sat a frustrated young man whose name everyone thought was Karl.

"Andy, can you get that?" Sheriff North called.

No answer. Just the ringing of the phone.

"Andy, are you deaf? Answer it!"

Nothing.

"He ain't here," Jared called, his arms jutting between the bars of his little cell. "Went out for burritos."

"Whadda ya mean burritos? Who ordered food?"

"I did. Got hungry."

Sheriff North, a short, stocky man in his early 60s with leathery skin, white hair, and riding boots, strode across the room shaking his head. "You're not supposed to tell my deputy what to do. You're being detained."

"Well," Jared responded, "being detained is making me hungry."

North rolled his eyes and picked up the receiver. "Stoneman Police Department," he said authoritatively.

Jared saw the man nod, then turn in his direction. "Yeah, he's here. Got him locked up. He broke all kinds of laws rushin' through my town like a bat outta hades. But I was just wondering why he had your number in his wallet."

The man nodded again. "Oh, I see. He's from your precinct and you know him. Well, looks like he'll be staying with us for a few weeks. You can come and get him then, if you like."

Sheriff North frowned, then smiled. "Why, yes, it is a strong, modern jail. Designed it myself. Why do you ask?"

The man lifted his chin slightly. "Yes, we pride ourselves in taking very good care of our offenders. We keep 'em safe and sound here in Stoneman. Haven't lost a detainee yet. We'll certainly take good care of young Karl for you."

Officer North paused. "What's that? You want to talk to him? Sure. Let me get the phone over to him."

The constable pulled out a wad of cord from behind the desk and played it out as he crossed the room until he stood by the cell. "A Captain Joseph Harrison in Washington, D.C., wants to talk to you," he said, passing the receiver through the bars while holding the phone snugly in his own hands. "Make it quick. This is long distance."

The prisoner nodded. "Sure thing, Sheriff. Thanks." He lifted the handset to his ear. "Hello?"

"Jared, what are you doing?" The voice on the line sounded tired.

"Well, hello, Captain Harrison. It's good to hear from you."

"What are you up to, Jared? Where are you going?"

"Yes. I'm fine. They're treatin' me just fine. Deputy's out getting burritos. I love burritos."

"Jared, listen to me. I know why they think

44

you're Karl. You took his wallet and his keys that night in the morgue. But you're not making it any better for yourself running away like this. You don't even have a driver's license, at least one that really belongs to you."

"Yes, I did have to explain that I shaved off my beard, but Sheriff North said the eyes were the same. He's pretty sharp."

The officer holding the phone smiled and nodded.

"Jared," Harrison continued, "there are social services programs right here in D.C. that can help you. You didn't have to leave the city."

Jared grinned broadly. "Well, thank ya, Captain Harrison. You be sure to tell all those nice folk on the third floor that I'm doin' just fine on my own."

"*You're in jail!*"

The teenager wagged his head. "Now, Captain, I got a roof over my head and lots of food to eat. I just may stick around for a few days. Or maybe not."

Sheriff North frowned slightly.

"'Course, that depends on the kind heart of my arresting officer. Mr. North may insist that I hold up here for a while." Jared smiled at the policeman standing on the other side of the bars. "I know one thing, I won't be drivin' my motorcycle through any more towns so fast. No sir, I done learned my lesson there."

"Listen here, Jared," the voice on the line pressed. "You're shovelin' it pretty deep right now.

That small-town constable may buy your innocence act, but I know better. You're out of your element, young man. You don't know how to survive in a civilized world. Ohio isn't the streets. There are nice people out there whom you can hurt. And there are not so nice people out there who can give you a ton of grief. Karl put my number in his wallet for a reason. He knew you'd do exactly what you're doing if anything happened to him. As a matter of fact—"

"No! You listen to me, Harrison," the boy countered, his young face taunt with sudden tension. "Karl understood about holier-than-thou police departments and how helpful city social programs can be. He knew about foster homes and juvenile detention centers and all those turn-a-perp-into-a-model-citizen projects. That's why he give me the Dream Seeker. And that's why I'm not going to stop 'til I'm where I'm going. You can try to catch me. You can try to run me down, but I'm faster'n you, Captain. I'm faster 'cause I got nothin' to lose."

"Jared. There's something you need to know about Karl. He—"

"He's dead. That's all I know. He stood up to that loser with the gun and got himself shot dead. End of story. Well, I ain't gonna die on some greasy street in no city. I ain't. This is my only chance, and I'm gonna take it."

"*Jared!*"

"Goodby, Captain. It's been a real joy talkin' to you."

The prisoner passed the receiver back through the bars and slammed it down on its cradle. "We're finished," he said coldly. "I ain't got nothin' more to say."

Sheriff North studied the young face staring back at him. "What're you runnin' from, boy?" he asked.

Jared lowered his gaze. "A lot of stuff," he said. "But mostly the streets. I'm runnin' from the streets." He kicked at the base of the bars. "I can't let 'em catch me. Never again."

Captain Harrison sat for a long moment, hands lying limp in his lap. He'd recognized the hurt in Jared's voice. Had heard it before, many, many times in the shouts and anger of young people caught in street crimes throughout the city. The sound was always the same, filled with sorrow and hopelessness, despair and rage.

But the overriding emotion always seemed to be guilt. Poverty and the street made you do things you normally wouldn't do. It turned your thoughts inward until survival became the motivating force in your life. Soon, your very existence became a question of him or me, my needs or his, my life or the life of someone else. All decisions revolved around the need to survive. Emotions such as compassion, tenderness, unselfishness, and forgiveness became buried deep within the soul where they ultimately died from mental suffocation.

Was that happening to Jared? Or was there still hope?

"Is everything OK?" Luella stood nearby, a cup of hot chocolate from the kitchen warming her hands.

Harrison glanced up, then shook his head. "No, honey, it's not. I've got a teenage runaway halfway to who knows where looking for who knows what!"

"Honey," the woman said, seating herself beside her husband. "Don't forget that you've got a problem right here at home—with Perry. He's kinda running away too. You need to help him as well."

The policeman nodded slowly. "I know. Seems I've got myself two young men who are hurting, huh?"

Luella smiled. "Yes. You do."

"OK. Then I'm going to do something about this situation."

"Which one?"

The man stood and faced his wife. "Both. I'm going to do something about both of 'em."

"How?"

"I don't know. But the answer's not here in the city."

"Where is it?"

The man narrowed his eyes. "When I took the promotion, the outgoing captain told me of a place he knew about, out in Wyoming or something, where there was this ranch for troubled kids. He said he was always passing out brochures and

48

stuff, trying to get sponsors for juveniles in the neighborhood. I got a feeling that Jared's heading that direction. That's why he wasn't driving south, but northwest. Ohio is between here and there. As a matter of fact, I remember seeing a folder on this place in the files at work. Yeah. The old captain showed it to me. Montana. It's in Montana!"

"Wait a minute," Luella interrupted. "I thought I heard you say something about the young man being in jail. Can't you just let him serve his time there, then have him sent back here?"

Harrison grinned. "This is Jared we're talkin' about. He uses jails like we use motels. Believe me, he can check out anytime he wants. Besides, he's not guilty of any crime I know about here in the District that would merit us having him shipped back at taxpayers' expense."

"So what are you going to do?"

The policemen walked to the door. "I'm going to go back to the office, find those files, make a few phone calls, and start my vacation."

"What?"

"Yup. I'm headin' west."

"But . . . but, what about Perry?"

The man grinned. "He's going with me."

Luella gasped. "You're taking our son with you to chase down a runaway?"

"Hey, some fathers drag their kids to Disney World. I bring mine along to track down felons. Besides, Jared isn't dangerous. He's just a confused boy trying to deal with the death of his friend and his past life on the streets. You know I'd never put Perry in any danger."

"Are you sure about this?" the woman pressed.

"I'm sure. I've got to do something or I'll lose both boys. And that would be a terrible crime."

Luella walked over to her husband and slipped her arms around his chest. "I love you, Joe," she said softly. "I'll trust that you're doing what you think is best. Just bring you and Perry back home to me in one piece, OK?"

"OK," the man said tenderly. "And maybe, in the process, I can find a home for Jared in this world too."

The captain placed a gentle kiss on Luella's lips, then slipped into his windbreaker, wrapped his gun holster about his waist, and headed out into the cool evening air.

☙ ☙ ☙

Jared shivered as the frigid predawn air rushed past him. Even though he felt extremely cold, he was smiling. In his mind's eye he could imagine a certain Ohio sheriff arriving at work to find that his modern, carefully designed, and completely escape-proof jail cell now held a new occupant. His deputy.

The late night maneuver had gone off without a hitch. First, he'd asked the dozing assistant lawman for a glass of water. A few minutes later he'd requested another. Then a third. The deputy had finally decided to make life a little easier for himself by bringing the amazingly thirsty prisoner a large pitcher filled to the brim with fresh water from the outside spigot. Since the container wouldn't fit through the narrow spaces between the bars, he'd opened the cell door. Jared, who'd used this ruse once before with a degree of success, happily grabbed the gift from the officer's grasp only to knock the pitcher out of his hands. A gallon of cold water had splashed against the constable, causing a moment of temporary blindness and breathless confusion. That's all Jared needed. By the time the deputy could see clearly again, he found himself to be the soul occupant of Sheriff North's jail cell.

Jared had unhurriedly retrieved his wallet and keys from the station desk while apologizing profusely to the drenched lawman, spent a few minutes in the back room looking for the keys to the fenced-in impoundment area behind the station, strolled out to where his motorcycle was parked, siphoned a tankful of gas from the department's cruiser, and after leaving enough money to pay for the fuel on the front seat of the car, had made his escape, slowly driving along darkened streets, keeping the sound of the Honda just above a low rumble. Once outside of town, he'd twisted the throttle and lunged into the night, leaving a wet and embarrassed constable to await the wrath of his confident boss the next morning.

Not long after the sun had risen to warm the earth, a phone rang in a modest home on the outskirts of Silver Spring, Maryland, and a sleepy police captain answered.

Luella awoke with a yawn as she heard her husband speaking into the receiver.

"He what? When? Oh my! Your deputy? Oh dear. Is the man OK? Good!"

The woman hoisted herself up on one elbow and laid her chin on her husband's shoulder, listening to the one-sided conversation.

"No. No, listen Sheriff North. We're going to track him down ourselves. Besides, I'm sure he's out of Ohio by now, probably halfway to Chicago. Yes. I'm taking on this case myself. No, he's not wanted here in Washington, but I've got a personal interest in this young man. He . . . he needs help. I think I do know where he's going. Montana. Yes, the one with the big mountains. I have reason to believe that's where he's heading. Of course, if I catch him, I'll bring him right back to Ohio so he can finish serving his sentence in your jurisdiction. That's only fair. Yes, sir, I know this is the first time anyone has ever escaped from your jail. It's still a record you can be proud of. And please tell your deputy that the people of Washington, D.C., apologize for the discomfort he had to endure at the hands of one of our juveniles. We're certainly sorry for what happened and hope he stops sneezing soon. That's right, you'll hear from me when I've made the capture. What's that?" Luella saw a smile spread across her husband's face. "Oh, yes, sir, we'll be careful with him. He won't get hurt. You're right, he's a nice young man in his own way. So you'll be hearing from me, OK? Good. Talk to you later, Sheriff North. Goodbye."

Harrison hung up the phone and sank back onto his pillow. "Jared checked out even earlier than I thought he would. That boy must want to get to Montana pretty bad."

"So, will you be leaving today?" the woman asked.

"No, but tomorrow for sure. I've got to work out some things back at the office before I go. You haven't said anything to Perry have you?"

"No. I'll let you break the good news."

"He's not going to like the idea very much, is he?"

"Probably not."

The man sighed. "Funny how, when a guy gets aimed in one direction, it's kinda hard to stop him."

"Oh, really?" Luella responded. "I wouldn't know about that. All the men in my life are so stable and predictable."

Harrison grinned. "Yeah. We are."

The woman chuckled, then rested her head on the man's chest. "What if he doesn't want to get caught?"

"Jared? Oh he'll—"

"No. Not Jared. Perry. What if this doesn't

work? What if it drives the two of you further apart? What will you do then?"

The officer lay still for a long moment. "I don't know," he said softly. "I just don't know."

Outside the bedroom window the morning sun rose higher, warming the leaves and the buildings, lighting the city for another day. Soon commuters would fill the streets, each in his or her own way running to or from what they believed to be their destiny. For some, the journey would bring happiness. For others, disappointment waited at the end of the road.

CHAPTER 3

Shadows

Jared sat sucking on a long, flexible straw, enjoying the sweet taste of chocolate on his tongue. Compared to the fast-food restaurants back in D.C., where it seemed you had to stand in line to do anything, the little eatery had the atmosphere of an empty baseball stadium with just a few customers enjoying a quick meal. No, it wasn't Washington. This wasn't even *near* Washington. He was in Bozeman, Montana, glad that his journey was coming to an end. After four days of riding and as many nights of shivering under increasingly frigid skies, Jared was happy to be anywhere that didn't boast a mile marker.

The little orange pup tent he'd purchased back in Virginia at the beginning of his journey had done a fair job of keeping out rain. But the cool winds and frost-tinged air that increased steadily as he moved north had ignored the space-age material of his shelter and settled somewhere unreachable in his bones. It usually took half a day for the sun to warm him enough so he felt more like a human being and less like an ice cube.

The seemingly endless flatlands that greeted him in Ohio had finally lost their hold on the earth's surface just beyond Billings. Jared saw the mountains coming, rising up from the prairie like proud sentinels, shutting out the sky with their lofty peaks and spiny pine forests. The mountain ranges seemed like magic curtains to the boy, drawing themselves back at his passing, presenting sweeping vistas and heart-stopping grandeur at almost every turn.

From his perch on the speeding motorcycle, he'd caught glimpses of strange curved-horn wildlife roaming the valleys and cliffs, giant birds circling overhead, mammoth beasts wearing what looked like shag carpets on their backs. Groundhogs regarded his passing without even a twitch of their tail. They just followed him with their eyes.

In the pass separating Livingston from Bozeman he'd seen an incredibly long train straining to reach the summit. Every sight was awe-inspiring, every view more wondrous than the one before. If he hadn't been so tired of traveling, he'd have wished that the road would go on and on and on forever. But the signs on the interstate announcing that the next two exits would land him right in downtown Bozeman itself were certainly a welcome sight.

Relief and regret mingled as he leaned into the wind and guided the powerful vehicle off the superhighway and soon found himself driving along Main Street.

Now he sat by the window of the little restaurant, gazing at the mountains to the east and north. Everywhere he looked, he could see vivid reminders that he wasn't on the prairies anymore.

As soon as Jared hit town he asked a few questions. The man at the filling station by the interstate had heard of Shadow Creek Ranch, but wasn't quite sure where it was located. The woman behind the counter at the antique shop across from the tire store said she knew of the ranch but suggested that he visit the co-op a few blocks away. "Most of the ranchers in the area do business there," she'd stated. "They probably can give you good directions."

A man in dusty coveralls and slightly torn flannel shirt had greeted him with a toothless grin. "Shadow Creek? Sure, I know 'em. Come in here all the time. Usually on Thursdays." He'd paused. "Hey, that's today. Why don't ya stick around? Old man Hanson usually shows up about 1:30. That's just an hour from now. If you'd like something to eat, there's a fast-food restaurant down the street. 'Course, food there tastes just like the junk they serve in California or Florida. Might not be the most nutritious fare, but it'll fill you up. You can get a bite to eat and then come back. Shall I tell Mr. Hanson that you're looking for him?"

"Ah, no!" Jared had responded quickly. "I'll just find the restaurant and come back a little later. See ya."

The boy put his burrito down and glanced at his watch. Quarter past 1:00. Almost time.

He noticed a battered flatbed truck pull into the restaurant parking lot. While he watched, an old man and young girl slipped down from the cab and headed toward the front door. They seemed to be in a lively conversation about something. Jared figured the younger of the two was probably about 12. A short crop of blond hair stuck out from under her western hat and her rosy cheeks moved as she talked. She wore riding boots, a pair of worn blue jeans, and a leather jacket covering an *I Love NY* T-shirt.

Her companion, a man in his late 60s, looked at home in his worn coveralls and straw hat. Both seemed enthusiastic about something. And both looked tanned and healthy, as if they lived or worked out-of-doors.

As they entered the building, Jared heard the old man speaking. "Honey, I'm sure Debbie will be happy that you're so willing to help out, but I really don't think she'll be any too thrilled with the idea of having Early in the ceremony. She's planning a wedding, not a rodeo."

"That's just it," the girl insisted, "she's having

a wedding on a ranch. A *ranch!* Ranches have horses, so there should be horses in the wedding."

The two put their discussion on hold long enough to order four bean burritos and a side of Mexican rice. The girl poured herself a glass of ice water and scooped up a supply of hot sauce packets from the condiments bar.

"What exactly do you have in mind?" the man asked as he retrieved a small pile of napkins. "Do you want Early to pull a wagon or something?"

"Pull a wagon? My horse? No way. I think he should stand up with the bride—you know, with the other bridesmaids. Tar Boy could stand up with Barry. It would be so neat! I'll bet no one has done *that* in a wedding before."

"I think you're probably right," the old man said with a chuckle. "Instead of a best man, we could have a best horse."

"Exactly," the girl enthused. "Then they'll know they got married Montana-style. The idea is brilliant."

After picking up their order, they made their way to a table by the window, not far from where Jared sat. The boy frowned. That youngster in the leather jacket looked familiar, as if he'd seen her before. Or was it just her picture? Wait a minute. Yes! Her picture. She was one of the smiling faces in the brochure.

Jared turned quickly and studied the battered truck parked across the lot. It was covered with mud and dirt, but he could just make out some letters printed on the door. Squinting, he studied their random outline carefully. Sure enough, with a little imagination he could just make out the words, *Shadow Creek Ranch, Bozeman, Montana*. He glanced back at the couple. They were the very people he'd been asking about. As luck would have it, they enjoyed Mexican food too.

"So if Debbie doesn't want Early to stand up with her, what can he do?"

The man Jared now realized must be the ranch owner leaned forward in his chair. "How 'bout if, when your dad walks Debbie up the aisle and Pastor Webley says, 'Who gives this woman to be joined with this man?' Tyler can say, 'I and these horses do'?"

The girl puckered her lips slightly. "I don't know," she said between chews. "Early is really hoping to take a more active role in the ceremony. He and that glue factory of Joey's are feeling a little left out."

Her companion sat for a moment savoring the spicy taste of his meal. "How 'bout if we had them as greeters? They could stand out on the lawn welcoming everyone to the ceremony."

The girl nodded. "Keep talking."

The old man stopped chewing. "I've got it. Early and Tar Boy can be in charge of the guest book. Of course, you'll need to be out there as well, showing people where to sign and stuff, but this

60

way the horses are actually on the program. We can list their names in the printed order of service and everything. It will say, 'Guest book: Early, Tar Boy, and Wendy Hanson.' It's perfect!"

The youngster nodded. "I think you're on to something here, Grandpa. Now if we can just convince my airheaded sister of our plan, we'll be home free."

"You just leave that to me," he advised. "I'm sure she'll see the value of having such fine livestock in her ceremony. Why, she should be proud that those two stallions even want to attend. Most horses could care less about who marries whom."

Wendy edged closer to him. "You're the best, Grandpa," she said with a smile. "Sometimes we even think alike."

Jared saw the old man frown, and then nod. "I guess we do. They say great minds run in the same vein."

"That's right," the girl stated. "Take your new old truck, for instance. I, like you, miss the old truck and am extremely upset that that stupid bear ate it." Jared blinked as his throat seized in mid-swallow. "This truck just doesn't have the same soul. It doesn't even *start* as often."

The old man lifted his hand. "Let's keep that little piece of information to ourselves, OK?" he said. "Your grandmother is still mad at me for not buying new. Why, new trucks don't have any soul at all. They just sit there looking shiny and perfect.

Who wants that? Give me a vehicle with a little character, a flaw here and there. I can relate to a truck like that. And you're absolutely right, nothing will ever take the place of my old one. Nothing."

The two sat in silence for a moment as if remembering a long-lost friend. Then they quickly finished their meal and gathered up their plates, napkins, and cups. "Just one more stop at the feed store," the old man said as they walked out the door, "and we'll be headin' home."

"I just know Debbie's going to like our guest-book idea," Jared heard Wendy say. "Imagine. She wanted a ceremony with no horses at all. What kinda wedding is that?"

The door swung shut and the teenager watched the two retrace their steps to the truck. At one point the girl noticed the shiny motorcycle resting nearby and ran over to have a look. The old man followed, and they stood admiring its clean lines and sleek profile. He saw the rancher study the license plate and then glance back at the restaurant. Jared turned his head and pretended to take another sip from his glass.

The ranch owner placed his hand on the young girl's shoulder, and they ambled over to the old ranch vehicle. After buckling themselves in and blowing a puff of blue smoke out the tailpipe, they drove away.

Jared hurried to the door and ran to the Honda. This was going to be a piece of cake. From here on out it was simply a matter of keeping the old truck in sight. He knew it would eventually lead him out of town and directly to his destination. But he had to be careful. Shadow Creek Ranch might be a welcome destination for troubled teens, but they usually showed up only when invited and after making proper arrangements. He didn't know how those people would react to having someone appear unexpectedly on their doorstep. For the moment at least, he'd play it safe and learn a little more about this strange family who were, apparently, planning a wedding that included horses manning the guest book.

With a smile Jared shook his helmeted head as he pressed the starter button by the throttle grip, bringing the engine to life. And he thought *city* people were weird.

.Ω .Ω .Ω

It was late afternoon by the time the truck pulled up to a big hotel-like structure hidden in a cozy valley formed by folds of the Gallatin National Forest. Jared, who'd been following the vehicle since it left Bozeman, guided his motorcycle off the gravel road and studied the distant scene, hands shading his eyes from the western sun. He noticed that the large dwelling rested beside a sparkling stream running the length of the valley. A small footbridge arched over the waters, and a well-used pathway led to a fenced-in pasture where horses grazed contentedly on warm autumn grasses. A shed and barn guarded one end of the enclosure while a stand of trees stood watch over the other.

He'd been careful to stay far behind the truck while on the highway. For the last five miles he'd followed its dust trail. Jared knew the occupants of the vehicle had no idea anyone was following them.

As he crouched behind the bushes by the road, he could see other people moving about the ranch, seemingly busy at work. A boy, about his age, maybe older, went in and out of the barn, carrying newly arrived supplies over the footbridge. He saw an older woman make her way to the truck, gather up several bags of groceries from the back, stand for a moment looking at the vehicle, then walk away shaking her head.

Edging closer, making sure no one detected him, Jared positioned himself on a hillside to the north of the big building. A younger man appeared on the upstairs balcony and waved at the girl he knew to be Wendy. She returned the greeting and motioned toward the pasture and shouted something about going to see Early. Then she raced across the footbridge and hurried through the open gate, almost toppling the boy burdened with a load of feed sacks.

The ranch seemed to buzz with activity—people running here and there, carrying things, talking to each other, laughing, or sometimes just gazing out over the expanse of mountains to the east and south. It was so peaceful even amid the tumult of activity. The air smelled fresh and pure. The sky hung blue and unpolluted overhead, like a newly painted canvas punctuated with cotton candy clouds and a brilliant sun.

Even the trees seemed to appreciate their surroundings, standing straight and tall as if proud to be a part of the valley.

Out onto the porch ambled a young woman with dark flowing hair and slender build. Jared's breath caught in his throat. She was beautiful—more beautiful than any girl he'd ever seen. "This must be Debbie," he said to himself, "the one who's getting married."

Sure enough, a man walking with a cane came up beside her and slipped his free hand about her waist. They spoke softly to each other while the late-afternoon sun outlined them both with a ring of yellow light, reminding Jared of a couple standing under a trellis atop a wedding cake in a bakery window. Even from this distance, it was plain to see that the two people were deeply in love.

The old man he'd observed at the restaurant climbed the steps and stood by the couple. All three gazed out across the valley. Suddenly the girl turned and spoke one word Jared recognized. "Horses?"

The boy stifled a giggle. The old man apparently had told Debbie of Wendy's plan for the wedding. By appearances, it didn't look as if she were accepting the concept with any degree of joy. The girl spoke the word again. "Horses?"

Jared saw Debbie's male companions discuss the idea between themselves. Then they presented their case to the girl once again, this time with much arm waving and encouraging gestures. It seemed Wendy had found not one but two advocates for her plan.

At long last, the girl nodded, but seemed to have some conditions for her agreement. After hearing her out, both men also nodded and left, leaving the bride-to-be standing alone on the porch. Before reentering the building, she glanced out across the pasture where Wendy was leading a handsome brown animal along a winding path toward the barn. Jared saw Debbie shake her head and say the word one more time. "Horses?" Then she turned and shuffled back into the building.

The boy studied the sun as it continued its journey toward the western mountain tops. It would be night soon, and if the recent past served as any indication, he'd have to find a spot somewhat sheltered from the cold to set up camp. He had food and several changes of clothes left in his bag, so he could stake out the ranch for at least another three or four days.

The last thing he wanted was to be sent back to Washington, D.C. Of course, he did have the little matter of Ohio to contend with. In that

state he was a wanted man, a fugitive from justice, a jailbreaker.

Jared looked around. No, this was too close.
They'd see his campfire. Besides, he was probably
on Shadow Creek Ranch property.

Then he remembered a dirt road turnoff several
miles back, between the ranch and the highway.
Yes. He'd follow that road deep into the woods and
find a spot where he could set up his tent.

Camping out was nothing new to the boy. He'd
been doing it all his life. Of course, in the city he
usually found shelter under a bridge or in abandoned warehouses. But the Montana countryside
had no bridges or warehouses here. Just trees and
mountains and rocks.

Jared hurried back to his hidden motorcycle,
then walked it the first half mile away from the
ranch. When he knew that no one would hear it,
he brought the engine to life and sped away.
Tonight, the woods would be his home. Tomorrow,
he'd discover more about the people who lived on
Shadow Creek Ranch.

🐦 🐦 🐦

"This is kidnapping." Perry sat, arms crossed,
staring out at the city lights as they flashed past
his passenger-side window.

"I'm not kidnapping you," his father laughed.
"You're my son, my own flesh and blood. We're just
going on a little vacation. I thought we'd get a four-

or five-hour jump on our trip before turning in."

"What about school?" the boy countered. "If you take me away, I'll flunk out for sure. You wouldn't want me to do that, would you?"

"We'll be gone only a couple weeks," the driver responded with a chuckle. "Besides, I talked with your homeroom teacher. She gave me some assignments for you to complete while we're on the road, so you won't get behind. She even said that me taking you to Montana is a great idea. Of course, I didn't say *why* we were making the trip. Your teacher mentioned that she wished more fathers would spend quality time with their kids."

"Quality time?" Perry chuckled. "This isn't quality time. This is kidnapping."

Captain Harrison eased into the traffic crawling along Interstate 495, the heavily traveled beltway around Washington, D.C. "Look, Perry. We've been through this before. I just want to spend some time with you, that's all. At home we're both so busy, our lives are jam-packed with school and work. We never see each other. Now we can. For two whole weeks—14 wonderful days!"

"Yeah, but it's not really a vacation 'cause you're huntin' down that stupid runaway. What kinda jerk would drive to Montana? He must be a real loser. Man, I'd head for California or Miami if I had a motorcycle."

"You would? Why?"

The boy shook his head. "Well, for one thing,

it's warm. And you're not gonna get buried in a blizzard or eaten by a wolf or somethin'. Another thing, you can't make any money in Montana. How many people have you heard about that make money in Montana?"

Captain Harrison shrugged. "None?"

"Exactly. Rich people, or people who want to be rich, head straight for Los Angeles or Miami. That's where the big bucks are."

"So you want to be rich?"

"Of course. Doesn't everyone?"

Harrison carefully switched lanes. "Not me. I don't want to be rich. I just want to make a good living, bring home the groceries, and pay the mortgage every month."

"Yeah, well, then you'll never make it big," Perry said with a sigh, as if he'd considered his father's financial situation before. "If you ain't gotta dream, you'll stay just where you are for the rest of your life."

Harrison studied his son's face. "Is that what you dream about? Making money?"

"Sure. I'm gonna to be loaded, you know, live in a big house. Drive a Lexus. You won't find me workin' at some useless job in a run-down police station—" He stopped suddenly. "I mean . . ."

"I know what you mean," his father stated. "You're not going to be like me, right?"

"No. I didn't say that."

"You didn't have to," Captain Harrison asserted. "And . . . I guess I can't blame you."

Perry lifted his hand. "You're a good cop, Dad. Really."

The man gazed out at the bumper-to-bumper line of cars. "I don't know. I might be an OK police officer, but I'm not doin' all that great in the dad department. I mean, look at this. The only way I can get my son to go on a vacation with me is to kidnap him."

Perry didn't respond. He just sat watching the traffic as it snaked along the beltway. Truth is, he didn't think too much of his father's work. After all, it snatched him away day after day, keeping him in the city for long hours. When he needed him, he was always gone. Weekends, evenings, even some holidays the story was always the same. Mom never complained. She'd always say, "What your father is doing is important." Yeah, sure. That was the one excuse that kept eating at his young mind. Whatever was occupying so much of his father's time in the city must be more important to him than his own son. Perry hated that thought, but it kept returning over and over again. It had gotten to the place where even seeing a policeman on the street made him cringe. The bad guys got more attention than the good sons who stayed at home.

Now there came out of the blue this Jared jerk who could make his father drive for days and days to some godforsaken state in the middle of nowhere when *he* couldn't even get the man to show up for a basketball game. *Let one street bum run off, and dear ol' Dad is hot on his trail like a coonhound baying through the woods.*

Vacation? Who was he trying to kid? This was police business—*official* business. It was nothing but the same old story, except this time he'd had to come along and get his nose rubbed in the very activity that kept his father a stranger to him.

Dad was right. He didn't want to be like him. No way! He'd find his happiness in big expensive houses and a cream-colored Lexus. Then he wouldn't have to worry about those idiots on the streets who stole guys' dads along with jewelry and VCRs. When he grew up, things would be different. Life would be different.

The little pickup truck followed the line of cars onto the I-270 spur heading toward Frederick, Maryland. His father insisted that he go along on this joyride to nowhere, but he didn't have to like it. In a couple weeks they'd be back in Washington and he could surround himself once again with things that really mattered—basketball, friends, and dreams.

🎩 🎩 🎩

Jared sat bolt upright, eyes wide with terror. They were coming. He could hear them in the hallway.

Hide! Hide in the closet!

71

Voices. Angry voices. They were saying something about his dad, about how he cheated them. His father's voice was thin, almost breathless as he tried to explain something.

Bang! Bang! The sound shook him with each percussive jolt.

Shouts. Running feet. A door slamming. Silence.

Wait. Don't go out. Stay in the closet. Don't make a sound. They'll hear you. They'll hear you!

Jared's hands trembled as he gripped the tent pole for support. *What's that? What's that noise? It's . . . soft, like breathing.*

The grimace contorting the boy's face began to relax. *It's pretty, the sound.* Soft like his mother's voice used to be. She'd sing to him—would hold him and rock him back and forth, back and forth in the chair that squeaked.

See? There's her face. She's smiling and brushing her hand against his cheek. *Listen to her singing. It's so soft, like the wind in the trees. Like the voice of the wind sighing in the branches overhead.*

Jared released his death grip on the pole and sank back onto his sleeping bag, body drenched with sweat, causing him to shiver in the cold night air. The wind. It had been only the wind.

He pulled the sleeping bag over his head and pressed the material against his face until the pressure hurt. The dream had come again. Or was it a dream? It seemed so real, almost like a memory.

Jared's shoulder's shook as tension gave way to tears. He felt so lonely, so lost. No one wanted him. No one cared about him. For a while, Karl had been his friend. But now he had no one to protect him. He had to run, to hide, to keep in the shadows like some fearsome beast afraid to show his face to the world because they'd catch him and put him in a little room with metal bars. It had happened before, many times. But he'd always run. He'd find a way to escape because they really didn't want him. They just needed someplace for him to be.

If people he met at gas stations, stores, and on horse ranches knew the truth, if they understood who he really was, they'd turn away. "You're just a street bum," they'd say. "A loser like all the others polluting our cities and town. You belong where I can't see you. Now, go way. Stay away. You're not wanted on my street, in my city, on my road."

But he wasn't a loser. He knew that. He was Jared, a boy who had no one to love. Just down the road was a beautiful home filled with people who cared about each other, but he couldn't join them. No. They'd send him back—they'd tell him, "This ranch is for young people who don't run and hide. You can be only a stranger here, a stranger in the shadows. Haven't you seen the pictures? Haven't you seen the smiles? Can you smile? No. You don't know how to smile so you must stay away or we'll be afraid of you."

The boy closed his eyes tightly. "I ain't a bad person," he sobbed into the sleeping bag held tightly against his face. "I wanna learn how to smile like those faces in the pictures. Please, somebody teach me. Somebody hold me and rock me back and forth, back and forth. I won't cry. I won't make a sound. Oh, please! I don't want to be a stranger no more."

The tiny tent hiding in the big woods fluttered with the passing of the wind. High overhead, far above the trees, the stars regarded the scene without emotion. They simply hung in space waiting for dawn's arrival like passengers at some cosmic train station.

Jared's sobs grew fainter and fainter as sleep recaptured him, pulling him into the stillness, shutting him away from the reality of the present and the terrifying images that haunted his past and his dreams.

A few miles down the road an old man stood on the front porch of a stately way station staring out into the darkness. He listened to the wind moaning through the trees and watched the stars drift slowly across the heavens.

His lips moved, forming words to a familiar prayer. Then he turned and reentered the building, leaving the night to the shadows, and the strangers who lived among them.

CHAPTER 4

The Loft

Jared settled himself as comfortably as he could among the bales of hay, making sure he was well hidden.

At dawn he'd driven along the gravel road to the spot where he could safely hide his motorcycle in the bushes. Then he'd scrambled down the embankment just as the unseen sun began to touch the eastern sky with the blush of a new day. Following the creek, he'd quickly skirted the big way station and stumbled through the dew-dampened grasses to the horse barn.

As he passed the house, a dog had begun barking, but he'd heard a young female voice call out, "Quiet, Pueblo! It's against the law to bark before the sun comes up." That seemed to do the trick, because the commotion ceased immediately.

Now he had snugly tucked himself into a small corner of the barn, up among the hay bales where he could watch everything that went on below and where, hopefully, no one would see him. He'd noticed a lot of activity in and around this structure the day before, so he figured this would be the perfect place to learn more about the people who inhabited the ranch.

Satisfied that all was well, he reached into his jacket pocket and withdrew his breakfast—an apple and a piece of peppermint candy. He also had a stick of gum in there, but decided to keep it for later. His other pocket contained lunch—five carrot sticks and an extra burrito he'd purchased the day before at the restaurant. As far as he was concerned, he was all set. Of course, there was one problem. His lofty perch didn't come with a bathroom. He figured he could slip into the bushes behind the barn if nature summoned him with any degree of urgency. There'd be no need to worry about any strange odors. The place smelled exactly like what it was . . . a barn.

He could hear horses milling about in their stalls and could see others out in the pasture standing like statues in the cold morning mist. The view from the loft out through the open window was tranquil—like paintings he'd seen on art store walls and in books during those rare occasions when he'd actually shown up for classes at the local public school. "You gotta get educated," Karl had told him many times. But it was hard to learn something when your stomach was empty. Besides, survival on the streets was a full-time job. Learning to read would have to wait for another time, another place.

On some days the homeless group he lived with ate like kings. On others, they had to spend many hours on the streets panhandling enough money to buy even a small meal. The cash reserve tucked away in Karl's secret hiding place where he'd kept the motorcycle had allowed the teenager the luxury of eating twice a day since leaving the city. Food, gas, and some much-needed camping supplies had drained that fund considerably. Jared figured he could eat for one more week and fill the motorcycle's gas tank one last time. Then he'd have to switch over to plan B. He hoped that wouldn't be necessary.

The sound of footsteps interrupted his thoughts. The boy lowered himself behind a bale of hay and waited, half-eaten apple in his hand.

"Early? Come here, boy." It was Wendy, the girl he'd seen at the restaurant. She entered the barn and shuffled over to one of the large covered containers by the door. Lifting the lid, she thrust her gloved fingers into a pile of what looked like brown seeds. Retrieving two handfuls, the girl closed the lid with her elbow and walked back to the door.

A small, brown horse galloped up to the entrance and happily munched down on the feed held out to him.

"You're in," she said, watching the animal chew.

"Both you and Tar Boy. Worked it out last night. We all can stand on the lawn and welcome everyone to the wedding. I'm supposed to tell people to sign some book with a stupid big pen with a feather stuck in it and hand out printed programs. Yeah, like they need a program to know what's going on. Debbie will say 'I do,' Barry will say 'I do too,' and they'll be married. How complicated is that?"

Early gobbled another mouthful of the feed piled in Wendy's cupped hands. "I don't know what the big deal is," the girl continued. "I mean, why even have a ceremony? They can get Pastor Webley to marry them without all the fuss. I asked Dad and he said to be properly married in Montana, all you have to do is go down to the Law and Justice Center on South 19th Street in Bozeman, get picture IDs made, have Debbie tested for rubella—that's some kinda gross and disgusting disease—and then she and Barry would fork over about $40 each. Some bozo would say a few words, they'd all sign a paper, and, bingo, end of story. Now, doesn't that sound like a whole lot less hassle to you?"

Early snorted, spraying feed all over Wendy's legs. The girl didn't even seem to notice. "My feelings exactly," she said.

More footsteps from somewhere nearby. "There you are," a male voice called warmly. "I thought I might find you out here."

"Hi, Grandpa," the girl said as the old man ambled up beside her. They stood looking out over the dimly lit pasture, drinking in its quiet beauty.

"We'll have a killer frost any morning now," the man declared. "Yup. Any morning. I can feel it in my bones."

Wendy brushed off the last of the feed from her hands and settled herself with a sigh in the entrance to the barn. "Grandpa, why do people have to get married?"

The old man lowered himself to the girl's side. "Love, I guess. When a man and a woman love each other, they get married."

"Yeah, but, why? Why can't they just be good friends forever. I mean, take for instance, Debbie and Barry. They go around like idiots hugging and kissing each other until I about barf. They give each other love notes and wink across the table and sit by the window with their heads together. They're always sighing and laughing at the dumbest things."

"They're in love," Grandpa Hanson said.

"So, why can't they be in love and not get married? Then Debbie can stay in her room down the hall from mine and Barry can live out here in the barn in the summer with Joey and everything can be the same as it is."

The old man smiled. "That would be all right for us, but Debbie and Barry want to be together all the time, to be part of everything the other person does. They want to *belong* to each other."

"Well," the girl said, "Early *belongs* to me, but you don't see us asking Pastor Webley to marry us."

Grandpa Hanson chuckled. "No, I don't, although the way you care about that horse, I wouldn't be a bit surprised at the request. You see, being friends is one thing. But Debbie and Barry want to be more than friends. They want to be what the Bible calls 'one flesh.' They want to join their lives on all levels—spiritual, emotional, and physical. I guess you could say that Barry wants to know what Debbie looks like the moment she wakes up in the morning."

"Hey," Wendy sniffed, *"I've* seen that. He's in for a shock."

The old man stifled a giggle. "What I'm trying to say is Debbie and Barry want to share their nights together too, to enjoy being man and woman."

Wendy gasped. "You mean, they want to have *sex?"*

"Yes."

The girl lifted a finger. "Does Dad know about this?"

"I'm sure he does."

"You mean, marriage is just so you can *sleep* together?"

Grandpa Hanson leaned back against the door frame. "They want to do more than that. Debbie and Barry want to *live* together, to spend their lives as committed partners, two people who've promised God and humanity that they will love and care for each other come what may. It's a very beautiful thing. God invented marriage in Eden when He made Adam and Eve. They were earth's very first married couple, and God Himself performed the ceremony."

Wendy tilted her head slightly. "So this marriage stuff is God's idea?"

"Yup. He created it so a man and woman could feel secure in each other's lives, knowing that they've promised to weather the storms of life together. God even says He'll help them keep their promise if they'll let Him."

"How?"

"Oh, He gives them loving thoughts, provides strength to forgive, power to overcome temptations, stuff like that."

Wendy thought for a long moment. "Is that why my mom left my dad?"

"What do you mean?"

"She didn't let God help her stay in love?"

Grandpa Hanson nodded slowly. "I think that's a pretty good description of part of what happened."

"So," the girl continued, "Debbie and Barry are doing what God wants them to do by getting married?"

"Yup."

Wendy nodded. "I guess that makes pretty good sense, except the sex part. That's still a little weird to me. But if Barry wants to start his day seeing what Debbie looks like when she wakes up, then I guess it's his funeral."

"I guess," the old man agreed.

After a long silence, the girl turned to her companion. "Grandpa?"

"Yes?"

"Do *I* have to get married someday?"

"Only if you want to . . . if you find the right guy."

Wendy gazed out across the pasture. "What will he be like?"

"I don't know. Tall, dark, handsome. That seems to be the standard nowadays."

The girl nodded. "Sorta like Early?"

Grandpa Hanson chuckled. "OK. But with a few less legs. And I don't think you'd want a guy with such a big nose. I mean, imagine if he caught a cold."

"*Gross!*" Wendy squealed.

"And I don't think you'd want your man eating hay in bed."

"No. No!" the girl giggled.

"And you might want someone a little neater in the personal hygiene area."

"All right. *All right!* I get the picture!"

Wendy and her Grandfather laughed and laughed, holding each other for support. Even Jared couldn't help but join in their mirth, burying his giggles in his hands.

After a few moments the two people seated at the barn entrance calmed down and grew silent. Wendy turned to her companion, her face serious once again. "Grandpa, just one more question. Will Debbie still be my sister after she marries

Wrangler Barry? Will she still love me?"

The old man slipped his arm around the girl's shoulders. "Honey, I can guarantee you that Debbie will love you as much as a sister can love a sister, maybe even more."

"I don't know," the girl stated. "She doesn't pay all that much attention to me lately. Now she's always talking about the wedding and how she and Barry are going to build a house up by some lake somewhere someday. I don't feel like I'm very important to her anymore."

Grandpa Hanson gently brushed blond strands of hair from the girl's face. "Well, maybe you should talk to her about how you feel. Maybe you need to remind her that you're still around and sure could use a little attention."

"You think so?"

"Absolutely. As a matter of fact, you could even ask if there was anything you could do to help her prepare for the big day. But you might want to leave horses out of the deal. We've already convinced her to have Early and Tar Boy manning the guest book. That might be all the ranch-type stuff she'll tolerate."

The girl sighed again. "OK. I'll see what I can do. I did have this idea for having Pueblo help Samantha with the flowers when she throws them down the isle, but I'll keep that to myself."

"Good," the old man stated while stumbling to his feet. "You can save up all your great wedding plans for *your* wedding day."

"Grandpa, I'm only 12!"

"Hey, Debbie was 12, and she grew up faster than a sunflower stalk in the spring. You'll be a young lady before you know it, and heaven help the boys in Bozeman."

"*Grandpa!*"

The two hurried away, throwing punches at each other and laughing, filling the quiet pasture with their joy.

Jared settled himself in the hay and took a bite of his now slightly brown apple. Grandpa Hanson seemed like a nice man, full of wisdom and good advice. A bit like Karl had been. It was plain to see that Wendy loved him dearly.

But who was this God he was talking about, the One who came up with the whole marriage thing? Was He really real? And could He actually help two people stay in love with each other?

The boy shook his head. Maybe it was something that the old man made up so Wendy would feel better. But if it was true, that would be neat. Imagine a God who helped people stay in love.

Jared sat chewing the sweet fruit, watching the sun rise above the distant mountains. Shadow Creek Ranch was full of surprises. He wondered what would happen next.

🐦 🐦 🐦

Perry threw his suitcase into the back of the

pickup and glanced over at his father who was coming from the motel office where he'd paid the bill and returned the room key. "Are we almost there?" he asked, a hint of a smile on his face.

Captain Harrison grinned. "What are you, 7? That's what you were always asking when we drove down to see your great-grandmother in North Carolina. Remember?"

"She made the best butter-bean stew," the boy stated, hopping into the right front seat. "And spice cake. I miss 'em. I miss Great-grandma."

"I know," the boy's father said, buckling his seat belt and slipping the key into the ignition. "She was one-of-a-kind. Loved to tell stories about the slave days, when her great-grandfather got snatched out of Africa. She ever tell you the one about the mule in the tree?"

"'Bout 500 times," the boy laughed. "It was her favorite."

"*You* were her favorite," the man said. "She thought the sun rose and set over you." He steered the pickup out of the motel parking lot and headed for the interstate on-ramp. "'You be shar ta tell dat Perry boy dat I'ze thinkin' on him today,' she'd say on the phone. 'You be tellin' him to makes sometin' of hisself. You hear? You be tellin' him ta study hard and don't sass nobody causin' if he do, I'll be comin' up dare to Washington, Dee Cee, and box his ears good, and I doesn't even mind if da president seez me do it.'"

Perry was silent for a minute. "Dad? Did Great-grandma want you to be a policeman?"

The man nodded. "She just wanted me to help people. When I was growin' up, she'd sit me down every once in a while and tell me, 'Now you listen heah, boy; da'is two kindsa folk in dis world— doze dat hep people, and doze dat don't. You be one a dem dat do.' I'd raise my hand and solemnly swear to her that I promised I'd always try to be one of *dem dat do*. I guess being a police officer is part of that.

"Funny, when I'm out chasin' a bad guy, runnin' down a dark alley, climbin' the stairs in some junked-out apartment building, I can almost hear her talking to me, giving me encouragement. She loved people and wanted everyone to live peaceable without violence and pain. Great-grandma had a great sensitivity to the needs of others. I'm proud that some of her blood flows in my veins, and flows in yours too. 'We'ze come from slaves,' she'd say, 'but now de only one we'ze gotta ansa to iz ouwselves.'"

Perry watched the flat Ohio countryside drift by. "I miss her," he repeated. "She was my friend."

The little pickup truck continued on its journey to the west, closing the gap between itself and the runaway with each passing minute.

🐾 🐾 🐾

During the morning three more Shadow Creek

Ranch inhabitants visited the barn. First came a powerfully built teenager, the one Jared had noticed working in and around the structure the day before. The boy went about his business with practiced precision, grooming the horses with a big brush, cleaning the stalls and filling them with fresh straw, then doing some repair work on a collection of leather straps lying across the workbench.

A huge black horse seemed to be his favorite. The teen spent an extra amount of time with the animal, talking to it, watching it eat, even asking it questions. "Must be Tar Boy," Jared said to himself, "Wendy's so-called glue factory. That creature would make a lot of glue!"

A short time after the horseman wandered out across the pasture, a little dark-skinned girl stumbled into the barn carrying a jar of bugs. Her companion, a dog she called Pueblo, stood barking up at the loft where Jared was hiding all the time he and the girl were there. The hound's companion told him to stop making such a fuss. "Haven't you ever smelled a rat before?" she asked. That comment made Jared a trifle uneasy.

Then came the man with the cane. He hobbled in and lowered himself wearily onto a wooden bench by one of the stalls. The young horseman returned, leading a sleek tan-colored animal by its harness. They clamored into the barn work area amid the clattering of hooves and steady stream of soft-spoken commands. "It's healin' up pretty good, Barry," the teenager announced. "See?"

The two bent low and studied the hind leg of the animal, poking around and gently rubbing an area just below the horse's knee.

"That stuff's amazing," Barry breathed. "Ol' Red Stone said it would work, and it does."

"What's it called?" asked his companion.

"Aloe. Aloe vera to be exact. It's juice from a plant. The Indian said his people have been using aloe to heal skin problems for generations. Guess it works on people *and* animals. Skin is skin, I suppose. So, Joey, the next time you catch your hind leg on barbed wire, you just glob some of this aloe on the wound and, voila, you'll be as good as new. 'Course you can't jump any fences for a while."

The younger boy chuckled. "I'll remember that when I'm out galloping around the pasture or pulling the wagon."

Barry laughed, then hobbled over to the table. Joey watched him carefully. "Bad today?"

"Yeah," the older horseman responded, reaching down and massaging his thigh. "Sometimes it's just a dull ache. Other times it's a royal pain."

"It's better'n being dead," Joey declared.

"Well, you're right there."

"And besides, if you were dead, you wouldn't be getting hitched up to Miss Debbie Hanson in a few days. That should put a little fire in your walk."

Barry grinned. "It does. She's certainly worth living for."

The two went about their work for a few minutes, then Joey asked, "So, are you scared?"

Barry looked up from the feed bin. "Of what?"

"Of gettin' hitched—you know, married, the ol' ball and chain act, taking the plunge, giving up the simple things in life, like . . . freedom and manhood?"

The older cowboy laughed. "Is that what I'm doing?"

"Sure. Marriage changes guys from strong, I-can-do-anything types to groveling Is-it-OK-honey geeks."

Barry laughed louder. "Oh, my! I didn't know. Tell me more."

Joey leaned forward, as if what he was about to say could offend a casual hearer. "I knew this guy back in East Village. Real tough character, know what I mean? Anyway, he falls in love with this female-type from Jersey and they get married. Flowers, cake, preacher, the whole nine yards. Then she moves in with him and the first thing you know they got curtains on the windows. *Curtains! Green ones!*

"I come over one night and say, 'Hey, Mike'— that was his name, Mike. Anyway, I say, 'Hey, Mike, how 'bout you and I going down to check out the docks?' Well, this big, tough street-wise guy looks at me and says, 'Sure, just let me ask the wife.' I mean, *excuse me!* Since when does a fellah have to ask a woman if he can go down to the docks?

"She says OK and we head for the river, you

know, to hang out and stuff, and he's checking his watch like every three minutes. So I say, 'Mike, you got an appointment or something?' He laughs and says, 'Nah, I just don't want to stay out too late. Nancy,' that's his wife, 'Nancy doesn't like to be alone at night. She gets scared.' Well, I'm thinkin' this is New York. You're supposed to be scared at night. Anyway, we head on back to the Village and it's like 11:00. I mean, the streets are just getting interesting. Mike says, 'Hey, gotta go. See ya.' Isn't that pathetic?"

Barry, who'd been politely listening to the story, nodded. "Do you know what your problem is?" he said with a smile.

Joey lifted his hand. "Hey, I ain't got a problem."

"Yes, you do," the horseman countered. "Problem with you, Joey, is that you've never been in love with a girl."

"Me? In love?"

"Yup. You see, it's not marriage that changes you. It's love. It makes you something you've never been before."

"No kidding?"

"And," Barry continued, "I know it's true because I've seen love change you in other ways."

"Me? Like how?"

"I've seen you become less focused on yourself and more interested in other things like . . . these horses, this ranch, the people who live here, and especially our guests. You've learned to treat folk with respect. Now, be honest. Are you the same Joey Dugan who roamed the streets of East Village a few years back?"

The boy thought for a moment. "Well, not exactly."

"There you see? And what made the difference?"

Joey turned and gazed out across the pasture. "I guess I became a little different when Mr. H and everybody let me be part of the family. They didn't treat me like a street bum. Everybody here treated me like a regular person."

"That's love, Joey," Barry said softly. "They loved you. Still do. Even Wendy loves you in her own way."

Joey grinned. "Her affection gets a little painful sometimes."

"But don't you see? Love makes things better. If you were to ask your watch-checking friend if he was more content roaming the streets with you or sitting across the room from his wife listening to a Yankee double-hitter on the radio, I'll just bet you he'd take the game over the docks any day."

Joey nodded. "You're probably right."

Barry tapped his cane on the floorboards. "I love Debbie," he said, "and I want to be changed by her. I want to become what she needs because I know she accepts me, bum leg and all. Don't ever underestimate the power of love. When you find it, hang on for dear life. There's nothing better anywhere in the world. Nothing. Not the street, not the docks, not anything."

As Barry hobbled to the barn entrance he leaned heavily on his cane. "Hey, Joey, I gotta go. I think I heard Debbie calling."

"I didn't hear noth—" The boy paused, then grinned broadly. "Yeah. I did hear her call. You'd better hurry."

Smiling, Barry started for the footbridge. Joey watched him go then returned to the workbench and attacked the leather straps once again. Jared saw him pause, look out over the pasture, then shake his head. "Me? In love?" the teenager mused. Then he chuckled softly. "I don't think so."

🐾 🐾 🐾

Captain Harrison hung up the pay phone and stood watching the traffic buzz by the filling station. He frowned as an uneasy feeling crept over him, a feeling he'd experienced before many times. But today it was especially disturbing. He may have been wrong about this whole trip, about taking his son to Montana. Worse yet, he may have been wrong about Jared.

"What's the matter, Dad?" Perry asked, ambling up beside the man, a bottle of orange juice in his outstretched hand.

The policeman took it and shook its contents absentmindedly, still studying the traffic.

"What's wrong?" his son asked again.

Captain Harrison turned as if seeing the boy for the first time. "Oh. Hey, thanks for the juice."

"Dad. You're acting kinda weird. Who was that on the phone? Is Mom OK?"

"Oh, yeah. Mom's fine. She says hello and that you're supposed to write to her every day."

"Write to her? We call each evening. Why does she want me to write to her?"

"OK. Whatever. Did they have orange juice?"

Perry blinked. "Dad. What's that in your hand?"

The man glanced at the bottle held between his fingers. "Oh. I guess they did."

The boy tilted his head. "Earth to Harrison. Earth to Harrison," he said, as if speaking into a microphone. "Come in, Harrison."

His father sighed. "I also just got through talking to my assistant back in D.C. He said Sheriff North called earlier. Seems we have a problem."

"Yeah? Like what?"

The police officer frowned, as if not believing what he was saying. "North said that when he checked his safe today, there was some money missing."

"How much?"

"'Bout $500."

"Wow!"

"But that's not my biggest concern. He said that something else was taken from the station."

"What?"

"A gun. A very powerful handgun. He said he

kept it and some ammo with the money in the safe."

"So? They got a quick-fingered burglar who was a little low on cash and needed some fire-power. They'll catch him."

The officer shook his head. "You don't under-stand. The money and weapon were there the night they brought in Jared, and no one has opened the safe since the boy escaped."

Perry blinked. "You mean—"

"Yeah. They think our runaway made off with the money and the gun, which means dear ol' Jared is not only driving without a license, he may be guilty of robbery and possession of a deadly weapon. If all that's true, our boy is in deep, deep trouble. And worse, the people around him may be in very grave danger. Jared has lost someone dear to him, he's running from the law, and has noth-ing to come home to. His emotions may be screwed up. Who knows what he's capable of doing."

The teenager frowned. "I thought you said you knew this guy."

"I do. Well, I know the Jared who followed Karl around like a shadow. But it looks like I don't know the Jared who's in Montana even as we speak staking out a dream, a dream he may very well turn into a nightmare for someone, including himself. The boy may be unstable, and an unsta-ble person who happens to also have a gun isn't something to take lightly."

Perry lifted his hands. "So, what're we going to do?"

"Well, for starters, I'm going to ship you back to D.C. on the next airplane I can find."

The teenager gasped. "Hey. Wait a minute. I don't want to go back. Besides, we've come this far. We're doin' the ol' dad-son thing, you know, gettin' to know each other. I think it's cool."

Harrison nodded. "It is cool. But being shot at isn't. I'm not about to put you in any kind of danger."

"Dad, you don't even know if Jared took the stuff."

"But what if he did? You could get hurt, or even killed."

The boy stepped forward. "Come on. I'll be OK. I mean, we live in Washington, D.C. I walk the streets all the time, and tons of people are packing guns. How safe is that?"

Harrison didn't respond.

"Besides, I've got one of the finest cops in the East protecting me." The boy glanced at his watch. "Look. We can get a few more hours in tonight, then hit the road early tomorrow morning. We can be in Montana before you know it. You can collar this jerk, I can look at the mountains, and then we're outta there. Piece of cake."

The man hesitated.

"Come on, Dad. Whadda ya say? Montana can't be anymore dangerous than our neighborhood in Silver Spring after dark."

"Well, you gotta promise to stay out of this," the man asserted. "I don't want you anywhere near Jared, do you understand?"

Perry lifted his hand. "I'm not even there. Scout's honor," he promised.

The man grinned. "You never were a Scout."

"Oh . . . well, then, I swear on my ancestor's slave bones. I promise."

Captain Harrison shook his head. "I'd forgotten just how persuasive you can be."

"Mom says I should be a lawyer," the boy stated. "That's OK. Lawyers are rich, right?"

The two walked to the car and got in. For each of them, the emotions of the trip had changed. Perry was beginning to enjoy having his father all to himself. It reminded him of how it used to be, before the promotion, before the late-night shifts and missed basketball games.

But for Captain Harrison, the journey had taken on a new urgency. If he got the Bozeman authorities involved, they could frighten Jared, perhaps causing him to become violent, or even scare him clean out of the state. Who knows where he'd go then.

For now the boy was where he could find him. The police officer just hoped he could get there before something terrible happened out on that peaceful ranch filled with innocent people. He knew he'd have one chance to bring the runaway to justice. One chance. If he failed, lives could be at stake.

CHAPTER 5

Somebody

Saturday morning dawned bright and cold. During the night the breeze had changed from crisp to numbing. Jared burrowed deeper and deeper into his sleeping bag, like a bear seeking out the hidden recesses of its underground cave.

Instead of slipping through the woods to the ranch as he had the day before, the boy waited with many other creatures of the forest for the brilliant, glowing orb to the east to warm the earth, chasing the cold away, loosening night's frosty grip on the land.

Jared ate breakfast encased in the tent, listening to the sounds of nature unseen beyond his protective enclosure. He heard a bird land nearby and scold loudly before flying away. A mouse or mole scratched at the entrance as if asking permission to come in. What he guessed was a deer walked gingerly past the tent before snorting a sudden warning and bolting through the underbrush.

The boy sighed. There was something peaceful about an early-morning forest, even a cold one. Back in the city it was usually a distant siren or car horn that drove sleep away. Often he'd hear someone being sick in the next room or suddenly awaken to a torrent of angry shouts. Here, nature spoke gently in a voice filled with feeling and energy. In the forest, morning crept reverently into your dreams like an invited guest and lifted you up with friendly, nonthreatening arms.

Jared took his time this morning, drinking in the sounds and aromas of the woodlands, basking in the serenity of his little campsite, allowing the sun to warm his body and his soul. The city seemed so far away, with its pain and memories. Here, among the towering pine, he felt secure.

The boy paused as he started to straighten up the confines of his plastic sanctuary. What would it be like to live here? What would it be like to awaken every day to the sounds of birds, wildlife, and the wind?

Just as quickly as the thought entered his mind, anger shoved it aside. No. It wasn't possible. Such a place was reserved for good people, teenagers who kept the law of the land, who did all the right things for all the right reasons. They deserved to be here. He didn't. After all, wasn't he on the run? Wasn't he an outcast? Didn't he have to hide, even now, from others?

Jared leaned his head against the tent pole

supporting the dome of his little orange world. Such a place as this could never be his. He was a street bum who could experience forest and meadows only from hiding places in barn lofts or from behind bushes beside the road. He wasn't good enough for Montana. He wasn't good enough for the mountains. He wasn't good enough for Shadow Creek Ranch.

Suddenly, Jared felt intensely lonely. His hands went limp in his lap as he listened to the forest beyond the confines of his tent. A familiar longing rose in his chest, filling him with deep regret. He didn't fit in. Wherever he was, whatever he was doing, he couldn't seem to make the world accept him the way he was.

Glancing down at his duffle bag, he saw the corner of the brochure jutting out from under a wad of dirty underwear. Picking up the colorful paper, he sat looking at the pictures—photographs of young people riding horses, swimming in mountain streams, climbing trees, racing along meadow roads in bouncing, jolting wagons pulled by powerful animals with Joey holding the reins. Everyone was smiling, their faces tanned and flushed with excitement. Oh, how he wanted to be in the picture! How he longed to experience their joy! Instead, here he was, hiding in the forest, afraid to reveal himself to others for fear of what they'd say or do. A worthless piece of humanity— that's all he'd ever be.

The brochure slipped from his fingers and fluttered to the tent floor where it lay among the remnants of his breakfast. Karl's reserves were vanishing. Soon Jared would be forced to begin living a life that would keep him on the run forever.

The teenager allowed his body to relax completely. He felt tired, sleepy. As the rising sun continued to caress the earth Jared slept alone in his little tent, surrounded by the forest, hidden from view by trees and the past.

🐾 🐾 🐾

Perry yawned broadly, covering his mouth with his fingers.

"Didn't you sleep well last night?" his dad asked, checking the rearview mirror for traffic before changing lanes.

"Sleep? With you across the room sounding like a wild animal park?"

The man grimaced. "I snored, huh?"

"Snored? I wouldn't call what you did *snoring*. It was more like your throat and your nose were locked in mortal combat with each other. How does Mom put up with it?"

Captain Harrison shrugged. "I guess she's gotten used to my strange noises. Some nights are worse than others—at least that's what she says. Sorry."

Perry sighed. "That's OK. Actually, I finally figured out a way to get to sleep, although it took me half the night."

"Oh yeah? How?"

"Well, I just pretend that we've left the television on and an old Tarzan movie is playing. Then, when I hear some new animal sounding like it's being attacked, I try to picture it in my mind. First thing you know, I'm dreaming about visiting a zoo. Works great."

The policeman chuckled. "You might want to share that with your mother in your next letter."

"Don't have to," the boy stated. "Already told her on the phone this morning while you were in the shower. She said she's tried it. Worked for a while. Then she started dreaming that she *lived* in a zoo. Now she just buries her head under her pillow or throws things at you."

"That explains it!" Captain Harrison gasped.

"Explains what?"

"Why I sometimes wake up with my side of the bed piled high with kitchen appliances."

Perry snickered, then burst out laughing. "And why it's hard to find the toaster some mornings, right?"

"Yeah, and why the can opener has a piece of my pajamas jammed in it."

The two sat giggling, trying to outdo each other. Harrison grinned broadly. This was the way it used to be—he and Perry laughing together, being silly, making jokes out of anything and everything.

He glanced over at his son. Perry's eyes were bright, filled with happiness. His face shown with

101

a peace his father hadn't seen for many, many months. He wished he could bottle up this moment and pass it on to other dads who'd allowed work and career responsibilities to crowd out their relationships with their children.

However, he was a cop. And he couldn't stop being a cop. He'd just have to find more ways to be a father again while keeping his obligations to those in authority over him, and especially to the citizens of Washington, D.C., who depended on him for protection. It was a tall order, one he knew he had to obey.

"So," the man said after the giggles had died down. "Tell me about school. How are your classes?"

"Dad," Perry countered, "we're on vacation, remember? I don't wanna talk about school. Too depressing. Besides, you've got me doing homework every night before we go to bed, so let's discuss more interesting stuff like . . . basketball, OK?"

"OK. No more talking about school. We'll chat about anything *but* school."

"Good."

The man thought for a moment. "So, how's your education comin' along?"

"*Dad!*"

Harrison laughed. "I'm sorry, Perry. I'm really interested. I mean, I've been so busy I don't even know what grade you're in. What are you, third, fourth?"

Perry rolled his eyes and sighed. "Dad, you're

not funny. You know very well that I'm in ninth! And I'm doing so-so in math and science, got a B in history, a B in French, and an A in P.E., although I almost got a B because I missed two games because of the flu."

"You got a B in French?"

"Si, senor."

The policeman nodded. "I can see why. That's Spanish."

"It is?"

"Oui."

Perry grinned. "We what?"

"We'ze goin' to Montana."

The boy nodded. "Yes, we is."

Father and son burst out laughing again as their little pickup continued along the interstate. A passing sign announced Minneapolis 60 miles ahead. They were well over halfway to their destination. Evening would find them in North Dakota. Tomorrow, Montana!

☙ ☙ ☙

Something was weird. The big way station stood deserted. Jared could hear no voices echoing across the broad lawn. He saw no activity out by the barn. Even the horses remained at the far end of the pasture, as if they understood that no one would greet them if they galloped to the gate.

"Where is everybody?" Jared asked himself as

he hung back behind the row of trees lining the creek west of the house and barn.

He saw the big farm truck resting by the kitchen entrance, and a car sat in the shade of the cottonwoods behind the building.

Wait, there'd been a third vehicle the day before, a red minivan parked out front. It was gone and, apparently, had taken everyone with it.

Jared wrinkled his nose slightly. Shopping? Perhaps. It was the weekend. Or maybe they had gone on a picnic or off to visit a neighbor. Hard to tell.

The teenager strolled across the empty lawn and slowly climbed the steps leading up to the porch. The boards creaked under his feet. At the top, he turned and glanced back at the valley. The view was breathtaking with towering mountains blotting out the distant horizon and massive groups of trees standing tall and proud everywhere he looked. No wonder he saw so many of the ranch inhabitants pause on the porch and gaze eastward. They were drawing inspiration from the panorama just as he was.

Jared listened for a long time, ears straining for any sound from within. Nothing. The ranch was silent except for the soft breath of the breeze and the far-off cry of a hawk.

He tried the front door. Locked. Reaching into his pocket, he withdrew a crooked piece of metal and inserted it into the knob. Click. The door opened at his gentle pull just as so many other doors had back in the city.

He'd have to be careful. The little red minivan could return at any moment. Jared wanted to be long gone before it pulled up to the base of the steps.

Not sure what he was looking for in the big way station, he knew he wasn't there to rob anyone. He wasn't there to fill a duffle bag with other people's treasures. Not this time. Instead he wanted to discover what made the people at the ranch so contented, so interested in each other. Maybe he'd find it here, amid the trappings of their lives.

Woof! Woof! Jared jumped at the deep-throated warning of an animal approaching from a dark hallway. He saw a mangy dog burst into the foyer, teeth bared, eyes focused on his legs.

"Hey, Pueblo, shut up!" Jared shouted.

The dog skidded to a halt. What was this? The stranger knew his name? Was he supposed to know this guy?

Pueblo sniffed the air, edged closer, and sniffed again. Oh, yes. He'd smelled that odor before, early yesterday morning and then again in the barn. None of the human beings who lived on the ranch had seemed overly concerned with the new aroma wafting about their living and working quarters, so the stranger must be OK.

The dog barked one more time, just to remind the visitor who was boss, then slunk back to his spot somewhere at the end of the hall.

Jared watched him go, then released the

breath he'd been holding in his lungs. "Good dog," he called, his voice a little shaky.

For the first time, the boy focused on the contents of the big lobby. He saw twin stairs curving up from the floor to a banistered balcony overhead. A large den and fireplace fronted the building, filled with comfortable-looking chairs and bookcases lined with colorful volumes.

Strangely, scattered about the place in random confusion were piles of white lacy ribbons, a curving arbor fashioned from painted wood, a padded bench, a table brimming with opened and not-yet opened gifts, another table burdened with a large glass punch bowl and rows of matching cups. Folding chairs leaned against each other along the walls, and assorted items he'd never seen before rested on unopened boxes and end tables.

Then he understood. They weren't bad housekeepers—they were getting ready for a big party, a wedding for Debbie and the man with the cane. That's what all this stuff was about. And it looked like the happy event would take place right here on Shadow Creek Ranch.

In the den he discovered envelopes and invitations, shiny shoes, colorful clothes hanging from makeshift racks, more gifts, several cardboard boxes filled with cloth, and a powerful cassette player with speakers.

A small wooden podium waited by the window. On it was a guest book, opened to the first page.

Across the top was printed in carefully formed letters "Wedding Guests of Debra Hanson and Barry Gordon." Below that line Jared saw a date and time printed carefully in colored ink. The boy glanced at his watch, checked the number indicating which day of the month it was, then gasped. The wedding was scheduled for tomorrow afternoon at 3:00.

Suddenly he heard the rumble of an approaching automobile. He ran to the window just as a red minivan passed by the house on the hillside road leading down the valley to the cutoff where the long driveway intersected it.

Jared hurried around all the waiting paraphernalia to the dining room and continued through to the kitchen. At the door, he paused and glanced over his shoulder. So this was what it took to be happy—a home filled with things that brought happiness. Isn't that what Grandpa Hanson had said out in the barn, that God wanted everyone to love someone else? Weddings celebrated the love of one person for another. These people understood that, and had filled their home with all kinds of things to make the celebration joyous.

The boy unlocked the back door and slipped outside. Then he jumped from the deck and scrambled to the protection of the bushes and trees lining the creek.

What was it like to love, and be loved? Jared wondered. Karl had said that love was nice if you could find it. On the streets there wasn't much to be found. Few cared about each other at all. Everyone was too busy just surviving another day.

It seemed so different out here on the ranch. But why should it be? Surely these people had problems too. They must have doubts and uncertainties. He assumed that they had to work hard to earn their keep, just like city dwellers. Jared knew that Joey spent hours in the barn cleaning, repairing, looking after the horses. The old man was never still as he kept the ranch running smoothly, gathering supplies, checking out the livestock, caring for the property. The women in and around the big house always had something in their hands as they rushed here and there. Everyone was involved in their own acts of survival.

The boy ran along the stream, thoughts rushing through his head in mild confusion. While it was true that, other than himself, not many criminals were sneaking about the place, he understood that nature could be harmful as well as beautiful. He was sure that the inhabitants of Shadow Creek Ranch had faced challenges from the very mountains, streams, and skies that inspired them day after day. The boy had seen and heard reports of forest fires, floods, earthquakes, and blizzards. So why was this valley peaceful when city streets had such sickening amounts of violence?

Jared shook his head. He didn't know the answer—he just knew he couldn't seem to figure out how to make the jump from one world to the other.

The teenager ran until he had placed a great distance between himself and the Station. He'd seen inside a place where love lived, and it looked bright and happy even in its confusion. If only he was good enough to be a part of all that. If only they would accept him into their circle. But they wouldn't. He knew it. They wouldn't because he wasn't smart enough or well-mannered enough or sophisticated enough to be a part of their world.

Bitter tears stung his eyes as he slowed his pace and walked along the stream. In the few short years that he'd lived, he'd experienced love only once, but he had been so young then. All that lingered from those misty days were scattered fragments of memories. Even they mingled with darker images. What had happened? Why had his world come crashing down around him?

Jared paused by the bank and lowered himself onto a rock. Sometimes he'd dream of a house with little rooms and brightly painted walls. As he slept he'd hear voices, soft and gentle, calling him by name.

He'd told Karl about the dreams, about the warm feelings they generated somewhere deep in his soul. His friend would always say, "Now don't go dwellin' on such junk. You'd better concentrate on reality, where your next meal is coming from. You leave dreams out of your life or they'll catch up to you and make you crazy." Jared didn't understand, but he figured Karl was older and wiser and knew more about life than he did.

However, the dreams and the feelings they produced wouldn't go away. They'd return from time to time, like strangers in the shadows, enticing him, calling to him.

Sometimes the dreams would turn dark and haunting. He'd wake up screaming. What did they mean? What was the night trying to tell him? How could he feel so warm and safe one moment, then have his heart stop in mid-beat as terror flooded his thoughts? It didn't make sense. Nothing made sense.

Jared stumbled to his feet as his stomach growled. He was hungry. Food waited for him in the tent back in the forest. Perhaps he'd feel better after he ate and spent some time in his little orange sanctuary.

The boy climbed the embankment and walked to where his motorcycle waited. He'd head back to the Station later that day, perhaps after the sun had set, allowing him to get close to the building. For some reason he felt drawn to the big dwelling in the valley, attracted to it by its strength and energy. While he was on ranch property, his fears seemed further away.

Jared slipped his helmet over his ears and adjusted the chin strap. He'd hurry back to the tent before any forest creatures figured out how to open his duffle bag and help themselves to his food supply.

With a twist of his wrist, he was gone.

🌙 🌙 🌙

The lights of Bismarck, North Dakota, shimmered in the distance. Traffic on Interstate 94 was light and sped quickly across the flat prairie land as Captain Harrison guided his pickup truck along the highway. Perry snoozed against the passenger-side window, oblivious to the fact that they'd traveled almost 100 miles since he'd fallen asleep.

Harrison squeezed his eyelids together in a repeated grimace, trying to bring a little more clarity into his vision. It had been a long day, but the bright glow ahead signaled that they'd soon be checking into a motel and enjoying the sensation of *not* moving for a few hours.

"Hey, Perry?" the man called softly.

The boy smacked his lips.

"Perry, wake up."

He heard the teenager draw in a deep breath, then expel it.

"Earth to Perry. Earth to Perry. Come in, Perry."

His son lifted his hand then let it drop. "Perry's not here. He's in Jamaica."

"Jamaica? What's he doing in Jamaica?"

"Lying on a beach watching girls."

Harrison blinked again. "Girls? Are you the same son who said he thought female-type people were a pain?"

The boy yawned broadly. "That was two years

111

ago, Dad. Now I think they're just fine, especially the ones in Jamaica."

The police captain chuckled. "I don't think I want to know what you were dreaming about."

"Her name was Philomena," Perry stated. "We were about to stroll along a deserted beach, hand in hand, with the waves washing over our toes."

"Philomena? The girl in your dream had a name?"

The passenger nodded. "Well, actually, Philomena sits in front of me in math class. She thinks I'm a dork. But, hey, it's my dream." Perry glanced out the window. "Where are we?"

"Bismarck. We'll find a motel and then get an early start tomorrow."

The teenager turned to his father. "Wait a minute. You woke me up to help you find someplace for me to go to sleep?"

"Life is just full of contradictions, isn't it?" the man declared. "Remember, we're on a budget, so don't try to talk me into anything with a pool."

The boy sighed. "Your idea of acceptable lodging is a place that's still standing when we drive away the next morning."

Harrison chuckled. "Why pay exorbitant prices when all you're going to do is sleep?"

The little pickup truck followed an exit ramp to a parallel street lined with motels and fast-food restaurants.

"Dad?"

"Yeah."

"What makes a guy like Jared become a criminal?"

The officer thought for a moment. "I've been in the cops and robbers business for almost 20 years, and the closest answer I've come up with is hopelessness. People, young and old, break the law because they don't have any confidence in themselves. They've lost hope."

"You mean, they get discouraged?"

"It's more than that. Law-abiding people get discouraged every day, but you don't see them holding up liquor stores or stealing company secrets from their bosses. They figure, 'Hey, I can work something out. I can lift myself back on my feet.' So they get busy and make something of themselves.

"Now, criminals on the other hand, I mean men and women who can't seem to break out of the mold they've cast themselves in, feel hopeless all the time. They don't see any way out. Thinking that the world is rejecting them, they turn to a life of crime as a way of surviving. 'Since no one else is gonna watch out for me,' they tell themselves, 'I'll just take care of myself, no matter if what I do is lawful or not.' Such people have little respect for the law. They feel they have no value."

Perry thought for a moment. "That's sad."

"Yes, it is," his father agreed. "Unfortunately, we all pay for their insecurities. We all become victims of their anger and hopelessness."

The boy pointed. "Hey, how 'bout that one?"

Harrison glanced at the motel on the corner. "Nope. Has a tennis court."

"We're not sleeping on the tennis court."

"Yeah, but we'd be helping to pay for it because they'll charge more for their rooms. Keep looking."

Perry sighed, then said, "So how do you give someone like Jared hope, or some self-confidence?"

"I don't know," the man admitted. "I usually deal with older felons. Sometimes they listen to reason. Sometimes they don't." Harrison turned to his son. "Where do you get your self-worth?"

The boy was silent for a minute. He watched a couple more motels slip by as he pondered his father's question. When he spoke, he seemed to carefully select his words. "I guess I like myself because Mom keeps saying how I'm so smart and handsome and junk like that. This Jared guy doesn't have anyone to tell him stuff—you know, to make him feel good. He's all alone."

"You're right," the man stated. "He's very much alone and doesn't know who he is or how he fits into society. That's a dangerous condition for a young person."

"Why?"

"Sometimes an individual who doesn't fit in tries to force himself on others and make them accept him. He or she can become violent in the process. That's my greatest fear in Jared's case. The boy's like a wound-up spring full of emotional tension and pent-up frustration. Twang! He could go

114

off at any moment. I just hope we get to him before that happens."

"How 'bout that one?" Perry asked, pointing out the window. "That motel looks like a dump, has no pool, probably's been condemned by the state of North Dakota, and is held together by duck tape and kite string."

Harrison smiled and spun the wheel. "Perfect," he enthused. "And the No Vacancy sign isn't lit yet either!"

"I wonder why," Perry said as the truck pulled up to a modest, clean row of rooms. He watched his father slip from the front seat and head for the office. OK, so it didn't look like a dump, but it wasn't anything near like the fancy places in and around Silver Spring. Policemen were such tightwads, working their tails off for a small salary. What fools!

The boy glanced toward the western sky where the last hint of day was fading away. Out there, beyond the horizon was a boy, lost in a world of his own making, alone among the mountains. For the first time since the journey began, Perry felt a tinge of sympathy for the runaway.

Tomorrow the two young people would meet face-to-face. Tomorrow they'd discover just how tightly wound Jared's emotions had become.

🐾 🐾 🐾

Jared wrapped his jacket about his chest and tried to make himself comfortable in the thick bushes by the house. He'd been here for almost an hour, waiting for someone to wander out for a breath of fresh air.

This was a bad idea, he said to himself. *It's too cold out here for anyone to lounge about on the porch. They're all inside sitting in the den enjoying the fire.*

He could see movement beyond the window curtains, shadows that rose and fell amid the yellow light filtering out onto the deck. From his vantage point halfway up the hill by the Station, he could see clearly the smooth, wooden surface of the porch and smell the hot breath of the chimney as, inside, a fire crackled in the hearth.

All at once, the front door creaked open and a long shadow fell across the floor. Then it closed again, leaving a dark figure standing in the moonlight. Jared recognized Debbie, the girl with flowing dark hair and smooth skin. She stood with a shawl wrapped about her shoulders, gazing silently across the pasture to the mountains beyond.

He heard her sigh. Was it a happy sound or a sad one? Jared wasn't sure.

The girl slowly crossed to the railing and sat against it, her face still turned to the valley. He could just make out her eyes and the gentle curve of her nose and cheeks, caressed by the silver light of the moon. Her hair shown like waves he'd seen on the Potomac as it skirted the city.

Such beauty. Such gentleness in a face. There was no hardness in her expression, no anger as so often seen on the streets of Washington.

"Debbie?" A voice called from the entrance as the door opened a crack.

"I'm out here, Daddy," the girl replied.

Jared saw a man walk from the light into the shadows. "Are you OK, sweetheart?"

Debbie nodded. "I'm fine. Just had to get away for a moment. Lot of commotion in there."

"I know," the man agreed. "Everyone's so excited about the wedding tomorrow."

"Me too," the girl said with a smile. "I've been counting the days."

Man and daughter stared out across the valley for a long moment. Jared saw Debbie slip her arm around her father's waist. "I love Barry," she said. "I love him so much."

"I know," the man said with a smile. "Although it's hard to tell with all that sighing and giggling that goes on whenever you two are together. And the hand-holding and snuggling? What's *that* all about?"

Debbie laughed. "I guess we don't exactly hide our feelings for each other, huh?"

"Not exactly. But I think it's wonderful. My little girl is getting married." He paused, then repeated the phrase as if saying it for the first time. "My little girl is getting married."

Debbie grinned. "Now, Dad, we've been

through this before. I'll *still* be your little girl. I'll *still* come to you with some of my problems. I'll *still* buy you ties for Christmas—"

"And you'll still ask me for money?" the man interrupted. "It just wouldn't be the same without that."

His daughter lifted her chin slightly. "Oh, I think between me and Barry, we'll make ends meet, sorta. I've got my part-time job at the mall, and he's been doing some consulting work on the side, teaching ranchers how to judge horseflesh. Or, maybe he'll be a teacher at the university. They've offered him a position in the Agricultural Department as a lab technician. Said they'd cover the costs of his getting an advanced degree. Wouldn't that be great?"

"Professor Gordon," her father said solemnly. "Sounds good. I know he'll be a success at whatever he tries to do."

The two were silent for a moment. "Daddy?" Debbie asked. "Do you think I know how to be a good wife? I mean, I want to be the best partner for Barry. He's the kindest, most wonderful man in the world, and I want to live up to his expectations."

The older man shook his head. "Listen, honey, Barry doesn't have expectations when it comes to you. That's what makes him so kind and wonderful. He loves you. He loves whatever you are or whatever you will become. You've known him for several years now. Have you ever seen him try to make someone something that they're not? No, he's not going to be making demands on you. He's going to accept you just the way you are. If anything changes—if you change—it will happen because you're *responding* to his love, not trying to earn it."

Debbie nodded slowly. "I just can't believe this is happening. I'm getting married. Me. Married. Mrs. Debbie Hanson Gordon. Has a nice ring, huh?"

"I like it! It'll be an honor tomorrow to officially welcome Barry into our family. He's been an important part of our lives since we moved out to the ranch. Now he's becoming our own flesh and blood. It'll be a pleasure to call him my son-in-law."

She snuggled close to her father. "Oh, Daddy. I'm so happy. Is it OK that I'm so happy?"

"I wouldn't have it any other way," the man declared. "Now, soon-to-be Debra Hanson Gordon, you get in there and finish preparing for your big day. I think I saw Wendy eyeing the arbor. She's probably trying to figure out where to hang a few horseshoes."

The girl laughed. "I wouldn't be surprised. Guess I'd better go in and protect what's left of my ceremony. I've already got two horses greeting the guests."

"I love you, sweetheart," the man said softly. "I'm proud of how you and Barry have shown us all how beautiful and pure love can be."

After planting a gentle kiss on her father's cheek, Debbie walked back into the Station, leaving the man standing alone by the railing.

Jared saw him gaze out across the moonlit pasture. A single tear slipped from the man's eye and left a silver trail on his upturned face. "Oh, God," he heard him say softly, "be with my baby girl tomorrow. Bless her new home. And thank You for letting me be her daddy."

With that, the man turned and reentered the building.

Jared sat on the hillside, hidden behind the bushes, lost in thought. Who was this God that everyone here seemed to know? Why was He so important?

A familiar longing flooded his musings. He felt lonely, cut off, abandoned. Everyone seemed to have someone else. Everyone seemed to be happy. Everyone but him.

Suddenly, a deep anger began building inside the boy, a rage that surfaced every so often, especially in times of great disappointment or loneliness. When it came, it almost blinded him with frustration and resentment. Why should he be the outcast? Why should others live in joy while he ran the streets, hiding from the law, living like a fugitive? It wasn't fair. It just wasn't fair!

He hadn't asked to be born—hadn't asked for the kind of life he lived. It had been dropped into his arms like a dirty, smelly garment. "Here, wear this!" society had told him. "Wear this and stay out of my way!"

Jared scrambled up the hill and began walking down the road, away from the ranch. Faster and faster he walked, then began running. "I'm worthless," he told himself between gritted teeth. "I'm no good to anyone. No one loves me. No one cares if I live or die. No one talks to this God about me."

Stumbling through the night like an out-of-control animal, he crashed through bushes and stumbled over rocks, blinded by angry tears.

He hated life. He hated people. He hated all those perfect people living on that stupid ranch. He deserved better. He deserved to be happy. Why should they have all the joy in life?

The boy skidded to a stop and sat down heavily on a rock to rest, his breath short painful heaves, fists clenched at his side, nails digging into flesh. Jared's eyes narrowed as he groaned out his frustration, his cry blending with the gentle sounds of nature. It wasn't fair. It just wasn't fair.

All at once he looked up, jaw set tightly. He'd show them. He'd show them all. Tomorrow would be that stupid wedding with all those stupid people running around loving each other. No, he wasn't invited. But he'd come anyway. They had no right to reject him. No right! And he wouldn't show up alone. No sir! He had a friend to bring with him, a friend that was powerful and spoke a language that everyone understood and respected.

That's right. Tomorrow he and his friend would roar down the road and turn at the driveway leading back to the Station. He'd make himself at home on the ranch, walking around in plain view, eating cake and cookies, drinking punch from those little glass cups, checking out the gifts on the long table with the white cloth draped over it. If anyone tried to stop him, well, he'd ask his friend to do his talking for him.

Jared stood and walked over to where his motorcycle waited in the bushes. Swinging his leg over the saddle, he inserted the key into the ignition. Pressing the start button he brought the vehicle to life. The time for dream seeking was over. Tomorrow would be his day, the day he stood up for himself and told the world that he *was* somebody. And everyone would listen.

With a throaty roar, the Honda and rider sped away, leaving the valley to the night, and to the excited inhabitants of Shadow Creek Ranch.

CHAPTER 6

Mountaintop

Captain Harrison laid the phone back on its cradle and sighed. It was Sunday morning—early. Very early. Shuffling to the window, he drew back the curtain a few inches and gazed out at the parking lot. Rows of cars sat in the predawn darkness, waiting to whisk their drivers and passengers to destinations unknown.

The officer glanced back at the sleeping form of his son who lay sprawled on his bed, blankets rolled in a heap at his feet. Ever since the boy had turned 4, he'd thrown off his covers, preferring to spend nights unburdened with excess layers of fabric. A semiclean T-shirt and pair of boxer shorts seemed all that he needed to satisfy him, even when snows framed the windows.

Harrison moved through the dim light and seated himself at the end of his own bed, lost in thought. How could he have separated himself from the boy? How could he have made anything—*anything*—more important than their relationship? Perry was his son, flesh of his flesh, bone of his bones! The very idea that he'd missed the all-important state finals basketball game filled the man with deep remorse.

His son wasn't a star player. No one chanted his name during a game. But he was a valuable guard on the high school squad, a guy on whom his fellow teammates could depend. To think he'd let him play in such a big meet without hearing his dad cheering from the sidelines caused a lump to form in the man's throat.

"I'm sorry," he whispered to his sleeping son. "I'm sorry, Perry."

The boy stirred, then blinked open his eyes. "Wha—? What did you say, Dad?"

Harrison smiled. "I said we gotta get up."

"Is it morning?" the boy asked, yawning, stretching his arms out in front of him.

"Almost."

"Almost?"

The policeman chuckled as he rose and headed for the suitcase propped open atop the dresser. "Well, in parts of New England it's morning. Come on, up and at 'em or we'll be late."

"Late to what?"

"You'll see."

Perry sighed. "Dad. You're not making any sense."

The man grinned. "Just get your skinny self into the bathroom and wash your face. Train's leaving in 15 minutes."

Perry gasped. "What about breakfast?"

"We'll get something down the road. Now, are you going to get up, or do you want me to carry you like I did when you were small?"

"Yeah," the boy chuckled, "I can see that happening. You'd hurt yourself."

"I would not," Harrison countered. "Why, I'm as strong as the day you were born!"

"In your dreams," Perry laughed.

Suddenly, he found himself being lifted out of bed in the arms of a grinning, straining man. "See," his father moaned, weaving drunkenly under the load, "I can still toss you around like a rag doll."

Perry looked at his dad, then at the bed below. "So why aren't we going anywhere?"

Harrison grimaced. "Because . . . I think I hurt myself." With a muffled plop, the boy landed on the sheets, a giant grin spread across his face. "Dad, I think I weigh a few more pounds than when I was 5."

"Yeah," the officer agreed, rubbing the small of his back. "Must be all those beans your mother fixes."

Perry rolled his eyes then bounded out of bed and hurried to the bathroom. "So," he called over the gurgle of running water, "are you going to tell me why we're getting up in the middle of the night?"

"Nope."

The boy splashed cold water on his face and

shivered slightly. "Is this Jared guy makin' a run for it?"

"Hope not."

"You just want to surprise me, right?"

"Right."

"OK. Sure hope it's worth all this trouble."

Captain Harrison walked to the window and gazed to the west. The sky was still dark. "I hope so, too," he said.

🐦 🐦 🐦

RRRRING! A phone resonated in the bedroom of a modest home in Silver Spring, Maryland. Outside, the sun was just beginning to peek above the horizon, sending soft, golden rays of light through the colorful leaves crowning the trees that shadowed the streets and cracked sidewalks.

Mrs. Harrison reached out, expecting her fingers to brush against her sleeping husband.

RRRRING! She searched the pillow resting beside her, then lifted her head. Oh, yes, her husband wasn't there. Hadn't been for days.

RRRRING!

The woman's hand moved to the phone perched on the nightstand beside the bed, bumped the receiver off the hook, and sent it tumbling to the floor.

Groggily, Mrs. Harrison pulled herself to the side of the mattress and began reeling in the cord like a fisherman hauls up a net. She placed the handset to her ear, frowned, then turned it end for end. "Hello?" she said, half coughing out the word.

"Mrs. Harrison?" The female voice on the line sounded far too cheerful for such an early-morning hour.

"Yes?"

"Hi, this is Ashly Peters. I work the night shift at the morgue in your husband's precinct."

"Yes?"

"Do you know how to contact Captain Harrison?"

"Ah, I've got the number of his motel in North Dakota."

"Good. Great! I need to talk to him."

Mrs. Harrison cleared her throat. "Is there a problem?"

"Well, not exactly. I've got some information he should know about before he finds that Jared fellow—you know, the runaway? Has he told you about him?"

"Yes."

"And, I wouldn't be bothering him with it except I just discovered a new file on the boy. It's different than the one your husband keeps at the precinct—you know, concerning his criminal activities. You see, I'm heading out of town with Dr. Milton for a coroner's convention in Florida, so I really need to talk to your husband before I go."

Mrs. Harrison tried to blink sleep from her eyes as she sat up in bed. "Ashly, I speak with my husband every morning before he sets out on the road. He'll be calling me in about an hour or so. If you'd like, I'll relay your message. That way you can get an early start on your trip, and we won't have to wake Joe up. They're in an earlier time zone. Would that work all right?"

A pause on the line. "Well, I guess," she agreed. "That is, if you don't mind. Got a pencil and some paper?"

Mrs. Harrison sleepily rummaged around in the nightstand drawer and withdrew a pen and small pad. "Yeah. I'm all set. What do you want me to tell him?"

She heard Ashly shuffle some papers. "I found this information mixed in with another set of records in Dr. Milton's office. He asked me to clean out his file cabinet, something that hasn't been done since Kennedy was in the White House. Seems our runaway's got some problems other than the fact that he's a runaway."

"What do you mean?"

"Well, according to this report, the boy experienced a series of . . . how do they put this . . . psychologically significant traumatic occurrences in his past. That means he's mentally screwed up. First event took place when he was 2½ years old. His father got into some kinda trouble with a drug ring here in the District. The police report, which was included with the coroner's write-up, says that a Dan and Merril Everett were confronted in their downtown apartment by two thugs who demanded payment of a large sum of money. When the couple couldn't deliver, the visitors pulled out handguns and shot them both dead on the spot."

Mrs. Harrison cringed. "Good heavens!"

"Yeah," Ashly agreed. "With friends like that, huh? Anyway, seems there was an eyewitness to the double murder, a little boy whom police found cowering in a closet. The report says the kid was as white as a cloud, shaking from head to foot. It took 'em an hour to talk him out. He was a mess."

"And?"

"Kid's name was Jared."

"*Our* Jared?"

"'Fraid so. Report said the boy went totally bonkers, would scream for days on end, wouldn't eat, threw up whatever food was forced down him. Can't say as I blame him, poor little guy. Social Services finally shipped him off to a foster home but, apparently, that didn't work out any too good either. Police arrested the foster parents for child molestation. Jared got bumped around like a bag of dirty laundry until he simply disappeared from the system about a year ago. Write-up says he ran away from his assigned facility. Your husband will know that's about the time he started showing up at the precinct on the shirttails of Karl Castanza, the young man who was killed before Jared left."

Mrs. Harrison felt an uneasiness in the pit of her stomach. "Is there anything else I should tell my husband?"

"Yeah. According to the file, Jared Everett has

a history of violent behavior and should be handled with extreme caution. He experiences mood swings and has been suicidal on more than one occasion. I thought Captain Harrison should be aware of these facts before he confronts the runaway. Hunting down a criminal always carries a degree of risk. If that criminal has a history of deviant psychotic behavior, it makes the job a little more spicy, if you know what I mean."

Mrs. Harrison pressed the receiver against her ear, trying to steady her trembling hands. "Yes, I understand."

"I would've told you sooner, but I just discovered this information moments ago. Jared's psychiatric history was jammed in with the coroner's report on his parents' death. Some clerk, who hopefully no longer works for the city, got a little confused. It should've been added to the current criminal activities file in your husband's office. Sorry 'bout that."

"Thank you, Ashly," Mrs. Harrison breathed, finding it hard to speak. "I'll contact my husband right now. He's got to know about this."

"Kinda figured as much," the caller agreed. "Tell Joe I'll be in the office for a few more minutes if he wants additional information, then I'm heading for National Airport and the sunny beaches of Miami. Sorry to wake you."

"That's OK, Ashly. Thanks."

Mrs. Harrison hung up the phone and reached

for the slip of paper resting by the lamp. She hurriedly dialed the number written across it. When a sleepy voice answered, she requested, "Room 23, please."

The lines crackled and snapped as the call was being routed, then Mrs. Harrison heard the electronic chortle of a distant phone being rung. She held the receiver against her ear and waited anxiously.

In a Bismarck, North Dakota, motel room a telephone rang, its jarring voice shattering the predawn stillness. The suitcase on the dresser was gone. The lights had been turned off. The parking space in front of the unit stood empty. The little pickup truck and its two inhabitants were miles away, speeding west, drawing closer and closer to the Montana border.

🐾 🐾 🐾

Jared heard the steady, gravely crunch of passing cars in the distance, signaling that the procession of invited guests was beginning to make their way toward Shadow Creek Ranch.

The sun hung high overhead, bathing the trees and rocks in pure, clean light. It was a beautiful day, a little cool, but perfect for an outdoor celebration.

The boy sat on a fallen log, listening. Everything was ready. He had carefully packed the duffle bag with food and clothing, rolled his sleeping gear up tightly, folded the tent, and cleaned the campsite and buried every piece of garbage. Jared wanted absolutely no trace of his presence to remain behind after he was gone.

Then he had firmly strapped his possessions to the Honda that now waited in the shade of a tall pine.

The teenager's anger had grown through the night, keeping sleep at bay. Now, as he lingered some distance from the road, he found himself kicking at an embedded stone at his feet.

After dislodging the rock, he stood and began pacing back and forth between the motorcycle and the log, mumbling under his breath. What he was saying didn't matter to him. The words made no sense. He just felt filled with energy, an almost uncontrollable compulsion to move about, like an animal in a cage.

Every once in a while he'd stop and glance down the forest path toward the road. "I'm coming," he'd say. "I'm coming." Then he'd begin stiffly pacing again, back and forth, mumbling.

Finally it was time. He didn't know why, didn't know what prompted the decision. Jared just knew it was time for him to leave the shadows of the forest and present himself on the ranch, in full view of everyone there.

He pressed a hand against the small of his back. A thick bulge met his groping fingers. Yes. He was ready.

Mounting the Honda, he jammed his head into

the helmet, turned the key, and pressed the start button while twisting the throttle. *Rrrrummph!* The engine barked to life. *Rrrrummph, RRRRUMMPH!* The bike responded quickly to his commands with its deep-throated growl. Jared loved the sound. It reflected perfectly the anger boiling deep inside him.

Lifting his left foot, he depressed the gear lever while squeezing the clutch with his fingers. The vehicle lurched forward slightly as the transmission engaged the drive chain. They had no right to keep happiness all to themselves. They had no right to exclude him from their lives.

As the roar built to a whine, Jared released the clutch and felt the powerful motorcycle lunge from the clearing. He lifted his feet from the forest floor and sped away, leaving the campsite empty.

"I'm coming," he repeated, his whisper lost in the shriek of the engine.

Joining the gravel road, he fell in behind a station wagon filled with well-dressed visitors. *Follow 'em*, Jared told himself. *Stay behind this car. No need to hurry.* When *I get there ain't as important as that I get there.*

A laughing child in the vehicle turned and waved at him. Jared didn't respond. He kept looking ahead, eyes locked on the road, ignoring everything else.

As the motorcycle and automobile passed above the Station, the teenager saw that the usually quiet, uncluttered horse ranch had become a scene of chaotic activity. From the elevated road he could see people and cars lining the driveway. Tables ringing the front lawn proudly showed off festive decorations as white ribbons and bows fluttered from every fence post. Brightly colored flower arrangements peeked from every nook and cranny.

White-painted stones formed a pathway from the Station steps, across the lawn, and through a gently curving arbor that guarded an area where dozens of folding chairs sat facing the footbridge.

The little structure itself had been transformed into a flower-encased monument, reminding Jared of some of the floats he'd seen in holiday parades. At the base of the bridge a soft, white carpet lay across the grass, and a little podium rose amid silver candlesticks and leafy plant stands.

At the head of the driveway, beyond which no cars could pass, stood two horses, their coats brushed to a high sheen, hooves polished black, soft tails and manes reflecting the warm sunlight. Wendy stood in front of them, guarding a small stand with an open book resting on top. She held a feathered pen out to the arriving guests, looking a bit uncomfortable in a pink-and-white dress with puffy sleeves.

Jared chuckled in his helmet in spite of his anger. Wendy didn't seem to be the type for frilly dresses with puffy sleeves. It was clear that festive occasions didn't suit her all that well.

However, he wasn't here to be festive. He was here to show the world that he was somebody, that they couldn't shut him out or keep him from the happiness that he deserved.

By now the car and motorcycle had reached the cutoff. Each turned and started back toward the Station. Jared slowed his vehicle and slipped it into an empty space not far from the road.

Once the bike was securely leaning on its stand, the boy laid the helmet on the seat and unzipped his jacket. With a final check of the lump pressing against the small of his back, he squared his shoulders, lifted his chin, and began walking up the driveway toward the ranch.

Like everyone else, the first person he met was Wendy, flanked by two horses. The girl looked at him, surveyed his jeans, T-shirt, and jacket, and offered a hesitant smile. "Welcome," she said, holding out the feathered pen and sounding a little like a recording. "Are you a friend of the bride's or friend of the groom's?"

Jared frowned. "Why do you wanna know that?"

The girl's smile faltered, then returned. "Well, if you're a friend of the bride's, I'm supposed to tell you to sit over there in those chairs to the left of that flowery wooden thing. But if you're a friend of the groom's, you're supposed to sit in those chairs to the right."

Jared lifted his chin slightly. "I ain't nobody's friend."

Wendy blinked, then cleared her throat. "Then

. . . I guess you can sit anywhere you want."

"What if I don't wanna sit at all?"

The girl stiffened and studied the visitor for a moment. "Then you can stand in the creek," she said coldly.

Jared moved closer, eyes narrowed. "What's *that* supposed to mean?" he asked.

"Nothing," Wendy responded without flinching. "I'm just telling you where to go."

"Hello there." Jared heard a voice behind him. Turning, he looked into the kind eyes of the old man who owned the Station and the land surrounding it. "Welcome to Shadow Creek Ranch," the gentleman said, adjusting his tie. He, too, looked a little uncomfortable in his own special garb—a three-piece suit. "I don't think I've had the pleasure of meeting you. My name is Mr. Hanson—Grandpa Hanson to most folk. What's your name and where are you from?"

Jared backed away a bit. "I . . . my name's Karl. I ain't from around here."

"Oh. Are you a friend of Barry's?"

The boy shook his head and frowned. "Hey, what's with all these stupid questions?"

Wendy leaned forward as if to tell her grandfather a secret. "Karl doesn't have any friends," she whispered. "Said so himself."

Grandpa Hanson smiled. "Everyone's got at least one."

"I don't," Jared stated, looking around nervously. "All my friends is dead, so just leave me alone. I ain't here to celebrate no wedding."

"Oh? Then why are you here?" the old man asked quietly.

The boy hesitated. "Just leave me alone. I ain't gotta answer your stupid questions. And you can't tell me to leave. You hear me? Just let me be."

Grandpa Hanson lifted his hand in warning, his smile fading just a little. "Listen, son, this is a wedding celebration. My granddaughter is getting married to my ranch foreman. You're welcome to enjoy the day with us, but I don't want any trouble."

"Hey, I can do whatever I want," Jared countered as the anger boiling inside him began to rise even higher. "This is a free country. I got just as much right to a good time as anybody." He thrust a finger in front of the old man's face. "I seen you guys goin' around actin' so high and mighty. I seen you talkin' 'bout God and love and junk like that. Well, that ain't the way it is outside this valley. So get real. It ain't like that at all."

Wendy moved closer to her grandfather, pen still in her hand. "Why is he saying these things?" she asked, genuine fear in her tone. The old man motioned for her to remain quiet.

"Besides," the visitor continued, "there ain't no God. There ain't no love. It's all just a bunch of lies."

"That's not true," the old man said quietly.

"Yeah? Well, where was your God when I

137

needed Him? Huh? Where was all this love garbage when I got shoved around like a stinkin' bag of horse manure? Answer me that!"

Grandpa Hanson lifted his hand again. "Jared, listen—"

"No, *you* listen. I ain't . . ." The boy stopped as his breath caught in his throat. "Wh'd you call me?"

"I called you by your name. Jared."

Wendy glanced up at her grandfather. "No, Grandpa," she whispered. "His name is Karl."

The teenager stood staring at the old man. "What's goin on here?" he breathed.

"You tell me, Jared. What *is* going on here?"

"How do you know who I am?"

Grandpa Hanson looked the boy in the eyes. "That's not important. What *is* important is why you're here and what you intend to do."

Unconsciously, the teenager's hand moved behind his back, his fingers searching for the thick, heavy burden jammed under his belt.

"Why don't we just go someplace where we can talk?" the man invited quietly.

"Grandpa," Wendy asked, looking first at her grandfather then at the visitor, "do you know this guy?"

"I know enough about him to realize he needs a friend."

Jared licked his lips as the old man continued to hold his gaze. He glanced about nervously. No one else was aware of the conversation taking place at the guest book table. However, other visitors were approaching, wanting to sign the register before joining the festivities.

"I . . . I gotta go," the boy stated, taking a step backward.

"Go where?" Grandpa Hanson asked. "Where do you have to go, Jared?"

A movement caught the boy's eye. Looking past the old man, he saw a little pickup truck slipping by a cottonwood tree. Behind it followed another vehicle, this one adorned with the logo and colors of the Montana State Police.

Jared glanced back at Grandpa Hanson, his face suddenly lined with rage. "You're just like all the rest of 'em," he growled. "You don't care 'bout me. You just want me off your land and out of sight so you can have your stupid wedding."

Grandpa Hanson, seeing the approaching vehicles, turned and spoke in a voice filled with feeling, "I do care, Jared. I care very much."

The boy gritted his teeth and locked the old man's eyes in an icy stare. "I needed you. I needed this ranch. Now I ain't got nobody."

The boy spun around and ran along the driveway.

Perry felt his dad bring the truck to a skidding halt and watched him leap from the cab, but not in time to catch a fleeing boy who sped by. The runner skirted the swerving police cruiser and raced on down the driveway.

"Get out!" Captain Harrison shouted to his son.

Before the boy could grab the handle, his door flew open and an old man wearing a formal suit jumped into the cab, wedging him back into the seat. "Hurry!" the unexpected passenger shouted. "He'll get away if we don't hurry."

Harrison hesitated, watching the teenager mount the distant motorcycle.

"Come on! Please!" the old man pleaded. "I know the roads. I know the places he might go."

The officer slipped back behind the wheel, pressing Perry even farther into the seat. He spun the truck around, sending wedding guests scurrying for cover. They roared past the police cruiser as it, too, executed a quick U-turn in the driveway before falling in behind the pickup.

Within seconds, Harrison was trailing the fleeing motorcycle as it fishtailed out of the trees and raced toward the cutoff, swerving recklessly around arriving cars and visiting ranch vehicles.

At the intersection Jared swung to the right and headed up the valley toward the distant mountains. "Yes!" the old man shouted. "He's heading into the hills, away from the ranch and the main highway. There are only abandoned logging roads up there. If we can keep him in view until he comes to a dead end, we've got him."

The speaker turned. "By the way, I'm Mr. Hanson. You must be Captain Harrison."

"Yeah," the driver responded, gripping the

steering wheel tightly as they plowed through a sharp turn. "Nice to finally meet you face-to-face. We've been talking on the phone for days now. And this is my son, Perry. He's not supposed to be in on this chase, and that's why he's going to promise to stay in the cab no matter what happens, right?"

The boy, wedged between the two large adults in the tiny cab, barely able to see out, nodded. "Sure," he gasped.

Jared leaned heavily into a corner, feeling the rear tire skid slightly. His wrist made quick, skillful adjustments on the throttle, controlling the power driving him forward at an alarming speed.

The boy's body shook violently as the motorcycle slammed into ruts and boulders scattered randomly along the mountain road. The Honda's engine howled, blending with the sharp, angry roar of the wind as it blasted past his helmet. He didn't know where he was going. Nor did he know where he'd been. He just knew he had to keep racing up this mountain, away from the ranch, away from the police car, away from Captain Harrison.

It had been a trick—a dirty, rotten trick! They'd known about him all along. Harrison and Hanson had been in contact with each other from the start, although the old man must not have revealed his presence to anyone else on the ranch.

Now the very men he thought would understand his longing to escape the city and find refuge in a land where teenagers smiled and laughed and slept peacefully under the stars—they were chasing him up an old logging road. The boy gritted his teeth in an effort to keep them from slamming together as the motorcycle jolted over the rough road. It was useless. He had nothing left to dream about. Nothing. Why go on? Why try anymore?

Captain Harrison gripped the wheel as he felt his truck skid outward before bouncing off the turn's thick, raised bank. The vehicle lurched forward as the bike up ahead raced on. His foot pressed the accelerator as the little pickup jolted onto a short straightaway.

"This is a city truck, not an off-road vehicle," he shouted above the metallic blare of the engine.

Grandpa Hanson braced himself for another sharp curve and felt his body being thrown against the door frame as the vehicle skidded sideways. "You're doing fine," he encouraged. "Looks like Jared is taking the Blackmore road. It ends on a plateau overlooking a long valley. When he gets there, he'll have no place to go."

The old man glanced at Perry, who remained wedged between him and his father. "You OK, young man?"

The teenager blinked. "Sure," he gasped.

Jared saw the road level out, then begin to climb again. He squeezed his knees together and tightened his hold on the handlebars. What was the use? If Shadow Creek Ranch had no place for him, there'd be no place for him anywhere. Life would be jail cells and cold, friendless streets. No, that wasn't life. That was death, only you were still breathing. Karl was the lucky one. He didn't have to worry about where his next meal was coming from, wouldn't have to hide anymore. He was free. He was safe.

Suddenly, the motorcycle burst from the forest road and sped across an open meadow high atop a flat plateau. In the distance rose more mountains, some with a dusting of snow covering their summits. The air rushing by was cold and clean.

Jared studied the far end of the expanse. He could see nothing beyond the meadow. It simply ended, falling away into empty space.

The pickup blasted out of the forest and sped across the open area, keeping the bike in view. Harrison's eyebrows rose slightly. "Hey! He's not stopping!"

Grandpa Hanson leaned forward. "Oh, dear Lord. No!"

Jared felt the bike accelerate, carrying him closer and closer to the edge. Yes. This was the best way out. He could be like Karl, asleep forever, never to know fear or guilt or sadness again. It would be so simple. He'd sail off the edge, drift for a moment or two, and then it would be over in a bone-crushing instant.

He thought of the woman who lived in his dreams, of her face smiling down at him, of her voice singing softly in his ears. "Mommy," he whispered as he shot forward, closing the distance between himself and the precipice. "Mommy. Hold me! Hold me now!"

In the tumult of his thoughts, amid the agony of his loneliness, he heard something afar off, like a distant call. The sound pierced his soul, his sadness, his anger. What was it? Who could be summoning him at his final moment?

The edge of the cliff raced toward him. He could see the valley stretching out to the mountains beyond. There was peace down there. It was the answer to all his longings.

But what was that noise, that piercing shout from behind? Was someone trying to tell him something? Was someone trying to call him back from the valley, back from the final sleep he deserved? He hesitated, his right hand releasing its white-knuckled grip on the throttle. The bike slowed slightly. Why was someone calling? Didn't they just want to hurt him, keep him hidden from view, away from the icy gaze of society?

Wait. What if they didn't? What if they were calling out in love, the same love the woman in his dreams offered so freely as she held him, rocking him back and forth during those long-ago nights that lived only in memory? Should he try just once more? Should he give whoever was calling him a final chance to fill the deep void in his heart?

Grandpa Hanson saw the bike turn suddenly, then begin to slow. After a long, sweeping turn at the edge of the cliff, it came to a complete stop.

Captain Harrison skidded the truck to a halt some distance away and saw the police cruiser come to rest beside them. As the boy straddling the motorcycle turned and looked back in their direction, the old man in the passenger seat lifted his hand from the steering wheel, letting the horn fall silent.

The two stepped out of the cab and stood by the vehicle. The cruiser doors burst open as the two officers jumped out, guns drawn and leveled at the distant form at the edge of the clearing.

"Jared!" Captain Harrison called, the word echoing across the high meadow. "Jared, it's time to stop running. Put the gun on the ground and walk away from it. Do you hear me, Jared? Do it now!"

The boy slipped off his helmet and shook his head. "It's all I got left, Captain. It's all I got."

"That's not true," the officer responded, his hands raised nonthreateningly by his sides. "You've got a future same as everyone else. But you're not going to enjoy much of it if you don't lose the weapon and let me take you back to Ohio." Harrison's voice softened. "You need help, Jared. You're messed up inside. You've been through stuff that's hurt you bad. Now you're getting even deeper in trouble with the law. It's gotta stop, and this is as good a place as any, don't you think?"

"Whadda ya mean, messed up inside?" the boy countered. "What are you talkin' about?"

"Jared. When I checked in at state police head-quarters in Bozeman, they told me my wife had called with some information I wasn't aware of. Got the whole story from my office back in the District. I know about what happened to your folks. I know about the foster homes and the abuse."

The teenager looked away, then back at the officer. "So what?" he shouted. "That ain't why you hunted me down. You just wanna throw me in jail for disturbing your friends in the District and for rippin' off that sheriff in Stoneman. That's your job. You're a cop."

"Yes, Jared. I am a police officer. And I did come after you because you broke the law. But that's not the only reason, especially after talking with my wife and hearing the complete file on you. Son, I came after you because you also broke my heart. You don't have to live like this anymore. There's good in you, Jared, but it's hidden under years of pain. Karl knew it. He understood."

"You leave him outta this!" the teenager warned angrily. "Karl's dead. That's all there is to it."

"No," the man responded. "There's more. You don't know *why* he died."

Jared laughed. "He died 'cause he was dumb enough to face down a banger with a gun. He deserves what he got—"

"But," Harrison interrupted, "the shooter wasn't after *him*."

Jared stiffened. "What do you mean?"

The policeman moved a little closer. "You know a guy named Preston?"

"Preston?" Jared chuckled. "He's a royal jerk. We hate each other's guts."

"I'm sure you do."

"So?"

"So *he* was the shooter. He was the guy on the street that night waving the gun around. Don't you remember?"

"No!" the boy called. "It was somebody else. Karl said so and told me to run back to the warehouse. That's when I heard the shots."

Captain Harrison edged forward a few more paces. "You're wrong. It was Preston in the alley, and he was out to get *you*. Karl saw him first and stepped in the way. He took the bullet that was meant for you. Do you understand? Jared, he died for you. Karl died for you."

Jared stood unmoving as the meadow grasses fluttered at his feet.

"Karl saw more in you than anyone else," the police officer pressed. "He believed that you had a future, that you could make something of yourself. So he took the bullet just so you could live another day and maybe, just maybe, get away from the streets. I couldn't let you run forever without knowing what he did that night. He loved you, Jared. Believing in you, he wanted to give you a fighting chance in life."

Harrison saw the boy's body slump forward as

sounds of anguish filtered across the open meadow. "Just give me the gun," he called, "and let me take you back. Spend your time in Ohio. Spend your time in D.C. Then begin living a life Karl could be proud of. OK, Jared? I want to be proud of you too."

Grandpa Hanson slowly walked up beside the police officer, then continued past a few steps. "Jared," he called, "I want you to come back to Shadow Creek Ranch when this is all over, after you've made things right with the law. I want you to meet everybody, ride horses through the hills, walk the mountain paths, visit these meadows. That's why you came to Montana, isn't it? That's what you really wanted. Right?"

He saw the sobbing boy nod slowly. "It's here for you, Jared. The ranch, the horses, the valley— they'll all be waiting. Promise you'll come back. OK? I'll ask Wendy and Joey and some of the others to write to you, send you pictures and stories about what happens here. That's why there is a Shadow Creek Ranch—to give you and others who've experienced pain a place to come when you need to escape, not from the law, but from yourself, from your past. Give us a chance to be your friends. You're always welcome here. Always. Whadda ya say, Jared?"

The boy slowly slipped off the motorcycle and reached behind his back. The two policemen standing behind the cruiser held their guns steady, sights centered on the boy's chest.

Jared brought his hand forward, letting the gun dangle harmlessly from his fingers. Captain Harrison ran over and accepted the weapon. Then the boy unzipped the duffle bag and retrieved a wad of money, handing it silently to the officer.

"Thanks, Jared," the man said softly. "I'm so sorry for what happened to you, about Karl, about everything. I just wanted you to know that. But you've broken the law and I've gotta take you back. Do you understand?"

The boy nodded, then lifted his gaze to Grandpa Hanson, who stood a short distance away. "Will you wait for me?" he asked, his voice trembling.

"We'll be right here," the old man responded, fighting back tears. "We'll always be waiting for you, Jared."

The two police officers hurried over and guided Jared back to their car. Perry saw them place him in the back seat, then hop into the front and start the engine. As the cruiser turned to drive away, Jared glanced over at him. Perry smiled. The prisoner returned his quiet greeting with a wave of his hand. Then they were gone.

The boy helped his father and the old man load the motorcycle onto the back of the pickup, securing it snugly with ropes. Then they left the meadow and drove down the mountain, following the winding logging road toward the valley floor.

"Dad?" Perry asked as they maneuvered slowly

around the ruts and fallen branches. "What's going to happen to Jared?"

Captain Harrison smiled. "Oh, he'll do his time in Ohio, then we've got some unfinished business in the District to clear up. We'll find a safe foster home for him and I'll recommend he undergo intensive psychiatric evaluation and treatment to help him deal with his past. After that, it's up to Jared." The man paused. "But I think he'll do just fine. He knows someone gave up his life so he could have a second chance. That's got to make a difference in a person."

"It does," Grandpa Hanson stated.

Perry glanced over at the passenger pressed in beside him. "Did someone die for you?"

"Yes," the old man said softly. "A long, long time ago."

As the little pickup truck continued down the mountain road, a wedding party waited patiently by the big Station. Some distance away, a police cruiser headed for the paved road. Inside, a teenager gazed out the window at the passing scenes. He knew that here on Shadow Creek Ranch he'd never feel unwelcome again. Instead, he was now an invited guest, someday free to roam the mountains without fear or guilt, free to laugh and shout out his newfound joys just like the people in the pictures.

Jared gently placed his hand on the window glass as if touching the trees with his fingers. "I'm gonna come back," he whispered. "Wait for me. I'm gonna come back."

A random wind rippled the leaves as if in response. Then the stately aspens and tall pines regained their composure, standing erect, proudly guarding the valley where love lives, where young men and women find hope for tomorrow and are strangers no more.

The Shadow Creek Ranch Series
by Charles Mills

1. Escape to Shadow Creek Ranch
Joey races through New York City's streets with a deadly secret in his pocket. It's the start of an escape that introduces him to a loving God and life on a Montana ranch.

2. Mystery in the Attic.
Join Wendy as she faces a seemingly life-threatening mystery that ultimately reveals a wonderful secret about God's power.

3. Secret of Squaw Rock
A group of troubled young guests comes to the ranch. Share in the exciting events that bring changes to their lives.

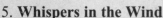

4. Treasure of the Merrilee
Wendy won't talk about what she found in the mountains, and Joey's nowhere to be found! Book 4 takes you into the hearts of two of your favorite characters as you see events change their lives forever.

5. Whispers in the Wind
Through the eyes of your friends at the ranch, experience the worst storm in Montana's history and a Power stronger than the fiercest winds.

6. Heart of the Warrior
Joey is about to face the greatest challenge of his young life. He's answered threats like this before. But never from an Indian.

7. River of Fear
A horse expedition brings Joey and Wendy face-to-face with the terrifying results of sin.

8. Danger in the Depths

Wendy Hanson is missing. Her father and friends frantically search. But every clue draws them closer to the unthinkable!

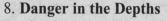

9. A Cry at Midnight
It's winter camp at Shadow Creek Ranch, and one camper's heart is frozen in pain. Exciting adventures help her discover a loving God who longs to heal.

10. Attack of the Angry Legend
It's more than 20 feet tall and is headed straight for the Station! Your friends at Shadow Creek Ranch are about to meet one of nature's most ferocious creatures.

11. Stranger in the Shadows
Stranger in the Shadows takes you on a mystifying journey from the alleys of Washington, D.C., to the valleys of Montana. You'll meet a boy with a frightening past who's searching for a Saviour.

Paperbacks, US$5.99, Cdn$8.49 each.

The Professor Appleby and Maggie B Series

Charles Mills and Ruth Redding Brand team up to bring you some of the best Bible stories you've ever heard!

1. **Mysterious Stories From the Bible**
Abraham and Sarah, Lot, Joseph, Rahab, Joshua, Hannah and Samuel, and Jesus as a child.

2. **Amazing Stories From the Bible**
Moses and the Exodus, Samson, Esther, and Jesus' miracles.

3. **Love Stories From the Bible**
Adam and Eve, Abraham and Sarah, Isaac and Rebekah, Jacob and Rachel, Ruth and Boaz, David and Abigail, and Jesus' first miracle.

4. **Adventure Stories From the Bible**
Samuel, Saul, David, Solomon, and Hezekiah.

5. **Miracle Stories From the Bible**
Moses, Elijah, Elisha, Joash, Josiah, and Jesus' miracles.

6. **Heroic Stories From the Bible**
Abram, Joshua, Deborah, Gideon, Jeremiah, John the Baptist, and Jesus' disciples.

Each book features challenging activities and is US$8.99, Cdn$12.99.